What a Rich Woman Wants

by

Barbara Meyers

What a Rich Woman Wants

Cover Art by *Kim Mendoza*

The Wild Rose Press, Inc.
PO Box 708
Adams Basin, NY 14410-0708
Visit us at www.thewildrosepress.com

Publishing History
Previously published: Samhain Publishing, Ltd., 2015
First Champagne Rose Edition, 2020
Trade Paperback ISBN 978-1-5092-3270-3
Digital ISBN 978-1-5092-3271-0

Published in the United States of America

"What do you want from me, Lesley? Do you even know? You keep me under wraps for months, but you dress me up and take me out when you need an escort to one your fancy balls. You can show up at my place in the middle of the night and sleep with me, but God forbid anyone should find out about us. You tell me your troubles and you act like you want my help, but at the same time…ah, hell." Niko shoved a hand through his hair and started back to the house.

"But at the same time, what?" Lesley caught up with him. She wrapped her fingers around his bicep in an effort to slow him down. Her grip was no match for the solid muscle it met, but Niko stopped anyway.

He stared at her in the murky light before he finally said, "But at the same time, this." He kissed her hard. She thought she could feel every muscle and sinew in his body as he wrapped her tightly against him. Abruptly he pulled away. "I am so damn in love with you, but as you've pointed out numerous times, we are worlds apart. So how are we going to make this work, huh? You can't tell me because you don't know. Because you don't think it can work. You know where that leaves me? Out in the cold. Without you."

Chapter One

Niko Morales navigated the interlocking brick driveway, lavishly landscaped on both sides, and parked his six-year-old, slightly battered black sedan under the porte cochere of the Robinson beachside estate.

Releasing his seat belt, he stepped out into the evening air, still hot this close to the gulf, but it wouldn't last much longer. In another month or so, the humidity would lift and the daily rainstorms would cease. The breathtaking heat that created near swamp-like conditions would give way to balmy breezes and cool nights. The sticky summer, complete with vicious mosquitoes and various other annoyances that full-time residents of Willow Bay lived with, would give way to "season." Full-blown tourist season, with its influx of snowbirds and vacationers, doubled the year-round population, overcrowding the roads, hotels, restaurants, and beaches. The local economy thrived while the residents groused.

This particular neck of land, not large enough to be called a peninsula, more of a wide finger, extended nearly two miles out into the Gulf of Mexico, forming a bay behind its mile-and-a-half width. The majority of the highly affluent in Willow Bay, people like the Robinsons, also owned homes "up north," though probably bigger and more impressive than these, used primarily for escape from snow and cold. Royal Cove comprised some of the priciest real estate in southwest Florida and boasted some of the most lavish homes as well.

Like this one, he mused, schooling himself to be unimpressed by the distinctive architecture, leaded-glass windows, peaked roofline, and wide marble staircase leading up to ten-foot-high, paneled oak double doors.

He liked to think he'd inured himself to the ostentatious displays of wealth he came into contact with nearly every day as a sheriff's deputy in Willow Bay. Money provided insulation from traffic tickets, DUIs, and the like. He'd learned some deputies were happy to take the cash and look the other way. He wasn't one of them and swore he never would be. He wrote the tickets and let the system do the rest. If a judge decided to alter the charges, reduce the penalty, or waive the fine, it had nothing to do with Niko. He did his job the best way he knew how and left it at that.

Still, a home like this was far from his own humble beginnings on the outskirts of Jacksonville. He reminded himself not to be intimidated. Wealthy people were still people with weaknesses and faults and problems like everyone else. Knowing this helped him behave as if he were on equal footing with potential sponsors, such as the woman he was about to meet.

Lesley Robinson ran her family's charitable foundation. She also, from what he knew, ran her family. Although this impressive estate belonged to her parents, she was the one in charge of a vast fortune. After a debilitating stroke her father suffered several years ago, Richard Robinson was cared for around the clock by a legion of private-duty nurses. His wife, Mitzi, remained the social butterfly she'd always been, perhaps more so now, unencumbered by her husband's presence.

None of that mattered, however, because Lesley was the one he needed on his side. She held the purse strings, and her support of the community center he dreamed of, one that would keep underprivileged young men off the streets and out of prison, would be the big push he needed. Lesley Robinson held sway in this tight-knit enclave of retired Fortune 500 CEOs, professional athletes, and self-made millionaires.

From the passenger seat, he picked up the folder he'd prepared, filled with information about the Challenge Project. A mission statement, cost estimate, and site development plan. As requested, he'd also included projections for annual operational costs once the center was complete and compared those numbers to the cost of keeping the same number of individuals in prison for a year. His goal was to develop these lost young men into law-abiding citizens, to give them the skills needed to hold down a job and raise a family. To be contributing members of society instead of a drain on its resources.

He knew it was a noble, idealistic goal and even though others had attempted the same thing in a variety of ways, he remained undeterred. He'd pulled himself out of a childhood steeped in poverty. He'd been sucked into a gang in his early teens, and he'd seen the damage such involvement did. He'd given up too much, including his own son, because at the time there'd been no choice. That's what he hoped to give other young men. Choices. One way or another, he'd get Lesley

Robinson on his side. With her help, he was confident the accomplishments he envisioned were endless.

He approached the front door, hearing a deep, melodic chime echo from inside once he'd pushed the bell.

In less than a minute, one of the doors swung inward to reveal a compact Hispanic woman wearing a uniform of sorts, consisting of a white polo shirt, white cotton slacks and white sneakers. Her dark hair was secured in a neat bun at the nape of her neck. She regarded him neutrally, neither welcoming nor repelling.

He greeted her in Spanish, introduced himself, and asked for Lesley Robinson. She returned the greeting, gestured him inside and closed the door behind him. She showed him to a small reception area consisting of two brocade chairs flanking an ornate table, over which hung a gilded mirror.

Niko took in the larger foyer, the sweeping staircase to the second floor with landings leading off in two directions. More marble and polished wood, the odd, echoey feeling of an excessively large home with few occupants.

He caught a glimpse of himself in the mirror, reassured he'd chosen the appropriate business casual look for the appointment. He'd shunned the one suit he owned for a long-sleeved white dress shirt and a navy blue sports coat paired with gray slacks. He would never be a suit-and-tie kind of guy, and one thing he'd learned in his thirty-three years was never to try to be something he was not.

He'd been blessed in many ways and tried not to take any of those blessings for granted, including his appearance. Due to his mixed race, or so he'd always thought, he was taller than many of his Latino peers. From the father he'd never met came not only his height, but his long limbs. He kept himself in shape with regular workouts. From his mother he'd inherited his olive complexion, dark hair—which he kept short and messily spiked—and brown eyes.

He had a small scar below his chin from his time with the gang. That was the only one visible when he dressed as he was now. There were others, though, along with a number of tattoos which were on display occasionally in settings other than this. They were part of him, part of his history. He didn't go out of his way to hide them, but he didn't flaunt them either.

In moments, the housekeeper returned. "This way," she said simply, and Niko followed her down a hallway to the right. She tapped once, opened the door, and gestured him inside.

From behind a massive desk, a woman rose and came toward him, hand outstretched in greeting. "Deputy Morales. Lesley Robinson. It's a pleasure to meet you."

He noted the long, slender fingers unadorned by jewelry, the nails her very own, neatly manicured and covered with clear polish. She was too slender, he thought, in her black pencil skirt that skimmed her knees and a long-sleeved, silky-looking blouse in a shade of teal which brought out the unusual bluish-green of eyes framed by unflattering glasses. Her hair was a mix of blond and sandy brown, swept up in a clip at the back, leaving a side sweep of bangs across her forehead.

"Come in, please. Have a seat." She gestured to the

two chairs in front of her desk. Niko chose one and made himself comfortable. "Would you like something to drink?"

"I'm fine. Thank you."

"That will be all, Lita." After Lita closed the door, Lesley indicated the folder. "You've brought some information for me?"

All business, he thought. No artifice. He liked that. Liked her, though he'd met her a mere thirty seconds ago. He handed her the folder.

She'd barely given him a chance to speak since he'd walked in the room. He didn't know why but he found her almost brusque demeanor refreshing. Maybe because he didn't particularly care for small talk, didn't see the point of it. He much preferred to cut to the chase. But it surprised him when others did the same, especially women.

She opened the folder and studied the contents, which gave him more time to study her and her surroundings. The desk was made of beautifully burled dark wood. Mahogany maybe. She kept it fairly neat, although there were some file folders and papers in a tidy stack. The other usual accoutrements. A multiline phone. A lamp. A computer.

A credenza sat behind her beneath a window that faced the front of the property, including the driveway. She might have seen him drive up. Maybe she'd studied him before he approached the house. It didn't matter. He had nothing to hide.

There were built-in shelves on two of the walls, some holding books, others displaying framed photographs or art. He noted a wet bar as well, with a small array of glassware along with decanters partially filled with amber liquid.

"Tell me about yourself."

He swung his gaze back to her. Lesley Robinson maintained a rather rigid posture as if she couldn't quite get comfortable in her own skin, even as she pretended to relax back into her chair. He wondered how long she'd been studying him while he'd been taking in his surroundings.

"I believe it's all there." He nodded toward the folder. "There's a copy of my résumé as well."

"Yes. Why don't you tell me what's *not* in the bio. Or the résumé."

"What is it you'd like to know?"

"Why this project of yours is so important to you. What motivates you. Why you care."

Wow. Cut to the chase. He'd raised some funds already from a few other sources. He didn't remember ever being asked why he cared or why this was important to him. Everyone assumed, as they were meant to, that he simply wanted to help his fellow man just as they did by donating money. No one asked about his history, how close he'd come to being one of those hard-core gang members if he'd stayed on the path he'd started down as a teenager. If he hadn't gotten out when he did, chances were good by now he'd be dead or in prison.

"I was in a gang when I was younger. I didn't think I had a choice at the time. I want to give young men who are in the same situation a choice."

"Elaborate on how you to plan to do that."

"Most of it's there." He indicated his carefully prepared folder filled with information, wondering now why he'd bothered. "Catch them young. No later than middle school. Keep them out of trouble and keep them in school. Offer after-school programs, help with homework, athletics, a place to go where they'll be supervised. Offer them counseling; teach them manners, basic job skills, conflict resolution. Include basic life skills training, personal finances, parenting. Help them learn how to be successful."

She regarded him steadily for a few moments. He stared back, feeling oddly at ease. She'd either use her family's charitable foundation and her influence to help him or she wouldn't. He could only do what he could do. He'd learned long ago his were the only choices he could control.

"How did you escape the gang?"

"After I testified in a trial against one of the other members, they rolled up the welcome mat."

"Why?"

"Because one member testifying against another is generally considered bad form."

A corner of her mouth lifted briefly. He noted her full lips and wondered what she'd look like if she relaxed completely. Smiled. Took off her glasses. Undid a button or two on her blouse.

She made no comment about his joke. "Why did you testify against another member?"

He shifted in his seat. Cleared his throat. Very few people knew the details of his testimony against Carlos Mariano. Even fewer knew he'd given up his son Fletcher in order to keep him safe from Mariano's retaliation and control. He preferred to keep it that way. By the time Carlos was sentenced to prison, Niko knew the best thing for Fletcher would be for his friends Hayley and Ray to adopt him.

"Why is all that important?"

Again, a corner of her mouth lifted. "Deputy Morales—"

"Niko."

She raised an eyebrow. "Deputy Morales, my family's foundation supports a variety of programs, as I'm sure you know. I decide which ones are worth presenting to the board of trustees. I don't work with people I don't trust. I won't see the foundation's funds misused. Building trust means gathering information about those who apply. So you can either answer my questions about your background, or I'll have Lita show you out."

"Haven't you already done a background check on me?"

"Of course. Do you want to answer my questions or not?"

"I testified against Mariano because he hurt a lot of people. He was going to hurt a lot more if he wasn't stopped. I was in a position to stop him."

"You were a gang member. Didn't you hurt people?"

"I was a minor player in a loosely organized gang of street kids. Carlos Mariano used intimidation tactics to keep the kids under his control. Since I'd grown up with him, I wanted to believe he listened to me, that I had some influence over him. Mostly I tried to keep him in check."

"But you couldn't?"

"No."

"I thought gang members took an oath of loyalty to one another."

How, Niko thought, could he ever explain his past

to a woman like this? Money insulated people like her from the harsh realities of the world. Private schools and limousines and yacht races were so far from the pothole-filled, drug-running, violent streets he'd been born into. How could he explain the loss he'd felt when the mother of his child overdosed on heroin? Or that fear of his own child growing up in such an environment drove him to testify against Carlos, to make sure his son got a better start in life?

"There are times, Ms. Robinson, when loyalty to an entity or to another person is tested, when you have to decide whether the price for your loyalty is more than you want to pay. That's what I had to decide."

He was sure he'd struck a chord. Her expression changed subtly, as if he'd surprised her or reminded her of something significant. She glanced at the open file in front of her. "You were never arrested, correct?"

"Yes."

"I thought an arrest record was a badge of honor to a gang member."

"I didn't want to be locked up for any reason. I was no angel, Ms. Robinson, but you're not going to hold it against me because I was smart enough not to get caught, are you?"

"Of course not. Thank you, Deputy." She cleared her throat, gave him what almost passed for a smile. "Niko," she acknowledged. She stood and extended her hand, so he did the same. "I'll see you out."

He followed her down the hallway, liking the sway of her hips beneath the skirt, even though she needed more meat on her bones. He couldn't help but notice how rigidly she held herself. She pretended to relax but never actually did. He wondered why she seemed so ill at ease in her own home.

She held the door open for him. "I'll be in touch about setting up a presentation to the board."

"Thank you."

The door closed decisively behind him. He breathed in the fresh air and let it out on a sigh. He reminded himself once again that he lacked control over what happened next. He opened the rear door of his car and laid his sport coat across the seat. At the same time, he became aware of the sound of a ball bouncing off the rear bumper of his car. He looked around for the source of it but saw nothing through the landscaping. A soccer ball rolled away from the back of the vehicle. He took a couple of quick steps to stop its progress. A small boy appeared several feet away when Niko scooped up the ball.

"Hello."

The child regarded him silently. Niko figured he was five or six years old. Dark hair, dark eyes, slender build. Both wary and shy, he looked ready to bolt at any moment.

Niko hunkered down to make himself less threatening. "This must be yours."

The kid stared and nodded, but just barely.

"Are you practicing your goal shots?"

He shook his head.

"Would you like to?"

"I don't have a net."

"Oh. My name's Niko. What's yours?"

The kid glanced over his shoulder as if expecting a reprimand from someone. "Ricky," he said, keeping his voice down. "I didn't mean to hit your car."

"It's okay. Is your name Ricky Robinson?" Surely

that couldn't be right, he thought.

But Ricky nodded. Was he Lesley Robinson's son?

****

Lesley wrapped her arms tightly across her chest and made her way back to her office. Once there she closed the door and sank into the chair behind her desk. By force of will, she relaxed her arms and shoulders, and rotated her head from one side to the other to ease the tension in her neck. She did her deep-breathing exercises, telling herself to relax, although she'd gone through some semblance of this routine less than half an hour ago in preparation for her meeting with Niko Morales.

She didn't like anyone to rattle her or for anyone to see they'd done so. If she wasn't in control…if she wasn't…well, what? Nothing good. She couldn't lose her head, her cool, her calm, her reason. She couldn't listen to her heart and make decisions on what it wanted. She'd done that once before, and the consequences were disastrous.

Instead, she kept everything on a tight leash. She'd been doing it for so long, holding herself, her family, her home, the foundation together, she'd forgotten how not to do it. She never let go, never relaxed. She knew from past experience if she wasn't vigilant, bad things would happen.

After a few minutes, she swiveled her chair to gaze out the window. The gurgling fountain just a few feet beyond the panes of glass and the view of the carefully tended landscaping never failed to soothe her. After closing the door behind Niko Morales, she needed to be soothed.

Yes, she'd done her homework on him, but a cold,

clinical background check hadn't prepared her for his presence up close. She'd trained herself not to react to men, or at least not to give any sign of her reaction. Though to be honest, she met very few who caused her to react in any significant way anymore. Most of the men she met were her father's age or older, his peers from the country club and the business community. They sat on the foundation's board. Some were family attorneys or accountants or old cronies of her father's or the husbands of her mother's circle of friends.

Lesley couldn't recall the last time she'd met a man in her own age range who sent a zing through her with just the touch of his hand. Maybe not since Steven, though she shied away from that thought. She'd been divorced from him for over five years.

Had it been that long since she'd had anything but a passing interest in a man?

In fairness, she'd been devastated by her husband's infidelity, an act he'd perpetrated right under her nose. She'd been forced to make quick decisions, to exert damage control to contain the chaos he'd created, and to protect the life of an infant.

But she'd never stopped blaming herself for all of it. For believing his lies, believing he cared for her. Most of all she couldn't forgive herself for making the foolish decision to marry him.

And then Maria's pregnancy happened, along with the complications. She remembered the young woman's fear for her son's survival. Even now Lesley didn't know how she could have turned her back on her pleas, especially in light of her pending deportation. The universe had been so unfair to the woman, Lesley wanted to do what she could to help.

Then the universe revealed its twisted sense of humor, and she learned who the baby's father was. Maria was deported before she could tarnish Steven's sterling reputation, and he refused any responsibility for the child he'd created with her. Lesley divorced Steven but kept the child. She'd made a promise to the young woman whom Steven seduced, then abandoned, to watch over and protect the son she left behind. And unlike Steven, promises meant something to Lesley.

A figure crossed her line of vision as she gazed absently out the window. Niko Morales had discarded his jacket and rolled up his shirtsleeves. He walked backward across the driveway before he suddenly dodged to his left and stopped, then kicked at something the landscaping hid from view.

Lesley stood to get a better look and saw a soccer ball roll back toward Niko. It looked like the one she'd given Ricky for his birthday last month. It had been a ridiculous gift, she'd realized after he opened it. Ricky didn't have many friends and no one to play soccer with outside of school. But it looked like perhaps he'd made a new one.

Niko spoke and gestured. Lesley shifted left and leaned closer to the window. Now she saw Ricky listening and nodding at whatever Niko was telling him. Niko kicked the ball and Ricky managed to bring it to a stop underneath one of his sneakered feet. Niko made a clapping motion and said something Lesley couldn't hear.

She tried to remember the last time she'd seen her son smile.

Chapter Two

The following morning Lesley made her way from her suite to the main kitchen. She'd slept poorly and needed coffee desperately. A lot of it. Lita would have it ready. She always did.

Even before she entered the kitchen, she heard Ricky chattering away with Lita. She knew as soon as she arrived he would clam up and barely acknowledge any conversation she tried to make. Lita had bonded with Ricky. It was Lita who cared for him as a baby, the one who got up in the middle of the night when even the nanny hadn't heard his whimpers. Although Lesley was legally his adoptive parent, Lita mothered him more than she did. She hated the way things were, but it was her own fault.

She braced herself as she continued forward, forcing a smile onto her face as she stepped into the kitchen. "Good morning, Lita. Good morning, Ricky."

"Good morning, Miss Lesley," Lita greeted her in her heavily accented but perfect English. Lita poured coffee into a delicate bone china mug and handed it to her.

Lesley took a sip. "Mmm. Thank you."

She joined Ricky at the table, where Lita had given him a breakfast of cereal and fruit, toast, juice and milk.

"How are you this morning, Ricky?" She smiled at the boy, who regarded her before addressing his reply to his bowl of cereal.

"Okay."

Lesley gazed out the windows at the side garden and the narrow strip of beach visible from here. She blinked, wishing as she did almost every morning that her life were different, that she were different. She sipped her coffee and glanced at Ricky once again. In so many ways he resembled Steven. Ricky's presence served as a constant reminder of Steven's treachery and her past foolishness.

But what Lesley berated herself for most was not getting over her own feelings enough to give Ricky what he needed—a loving mother figure. She simply couldn't do it. His eyes were dark like Maria's, and they seemed to judge her and find her wanting. Thank God for Lita, she thought, just as the other woman set a plate with a slice of plain whole-grain toast in front of her. She gave Lita a weak smile and a thank-you. Lita replied by topping off Lesley's cup.

"Hello, darlings." Lesley's mother glided into the room, wearing one of her beaded peignoirs, this one a delicate shade of lavender that matched the feathered high-heeled slippers on her feet.

"Good morning, Mother."

"Hi, Missy," Ricky said, glancing her way before taking another bite of toast. He'd not been able to get his tongue around "Mitzi" when he'd started to talk and invariably said "Missy" instead. Mitzi Robinson would never be referred to as Nana or Grandma. The title he'd given to his surrogate grandmother stuck.

"How's my little man this morning?" From behind she placed a hand on either side of Ricky's head and dropped a kiss on his dark hair as she took a seat at the table. "Ready for school?"

"Yes, ma'am," Ricky replied glumly.

"Thank you, Lita," Mitzi said as coffee appeared in front of her along with a cup filled with delicate wedges of ruby red grapefruit.

Lesley sipped more coffee, regarding both her mother and Ricky as they addressed their breakfasts. It never ceased to amaze her that Mitzi so willingly accepted Ricky into her household. Lesley hadn't expected her age- and appearance-conscious mother to allow a child with technically no blood relation to her to be considered her grandchild.

Yet for all her flightiness and fluff, Mitzi had a special relationship with Ricky. Though she'd allowed Lita to do the dirty work of changing diapers and fixing formula once the infant had been released from the hospital, it was Mitzi who rocked him and soothed him with a tenderness Lesley hadn't known her capable of. In the evenings she read to him, often until he fell asleep. On Sunday afternoons, she sometimes took him out for ice cream or to a movie.

Lesley couldn't be sure if Ricky provided a respite from Mitzi's loneliness or if her mother truly cared for the child. A small part of her was jealous, too, for she couldn't remember Mitzi ever being so interested in her when she'd been Ricky's age.

"How's Dad this morning?" she asked once Ricky finished his meal and went to brush his teeth at Lita's insistence.

"In a mood," Mitzi replied. She'd finished her grapefruit and pushed the bowl away. As if on cue, Lita refilled her coffee cup. Mitzi added a yellow packet of sweetener and a drop of cream. "But then he's always in a mood. It's no wonder, considering how long it takes him to write even a sentence."

Uh-oh. Her father wasn't having a good morning. Although normally Mitzi carried on as if her spouse's absence didn't faze her, there were days when her frustration and sadness got the better of her.

"I'll go up and see him later." Lesley visited her father every morning, so she didn't need to mention it, but she had so little to say to her mother. Her father's condition didn't change significantly from day to day. A rotating crew of private-duty nurses and physical and speech therapists attended to his every need. Six years after his stroke, he'd made little progress. He couldn't speak, couldn't walk or feed himself. Lesley often thought it must be hell on earth to be trapped in a body one had so little control over. But money was no object. Richard Robinson received the best care available, and with the help of the latest in high-tech computer interface assistance, he was slowly writing his memoir.

"I don't know why you spend so much time with him," Mitzi said with a sigh as she gazed out the window. "Some days I don't think he appreciates it."

"You don't know that."

A daddy's girl her whole life, Lesley supposed she still was. It was Richard who had encouraged her, Richard she'd spent time with as a child, although in truth much of their quality time together occurred in his office. She'd listened and learned. Even while she'd colored or read or worked on puzzles, a part of her absorbed his business sense. It was no surprise that everything he'd taught her, along with what her Wharton MBA offered, had prepared her to take over when he'd been unable to continue as CEO of the

Robinson Group.

He'd already shifted into the role of chairman of the board before the stroke, leaving the day-to-day operations to his hand-picked executive staff. Lesley took over his role and worked mostly from her home office. She traveled to board meetings a few times a year and also oversaw the charitable foundation.

Some days, she almost convinced herself it was enough. But late at night, she felt the emptiness of her life.

Chapter Three

Niko unlocked his front door and stepped inside. His gaze swept the space before him. A living room opened into a dining area and the kitchen beyond. Niko Morales, homeowner. In his wildest dreams he'd never thought he might one day have a place of his own. It wasn't much of a place, a fixer-upper he'd been lucky to snatch up from the foreclosure vultures six months ago. *Fixer-upper* was putting it kindly. The place was a dump. But the structure was solid and he saw its potential. That's what Niko told himself, although he didn't have the money or the time to do much work on it. Instead he settled for painting and patching and keeping it clean.

It was his and that's what he cared about. The aesthetics weren't important at the moment. He unbuckled his belt, removed his weapon and locked it in the gun safe he kept on the top shelf of the tiny closet near the front door.

He yanked off his uniform shirt and the tee underneath as he headed toward the bathroom, tossing them into the laundry basket. He turned on the shower before he shed the rest of his clothes. Stepping under the warm spray brought nothing but relief. His shift was over and he wasn't on duty again for two days. His growling stomach made him consider going to Señor Tequilas for dinner. The beer was cheap, chips and salsa were free and the enchiladas were some of the best he'd ever eaten. A quick mental calculation about the state of his finances until payday told him he could afford a meal out.

He wrapped a towel around his waist and went into the bedroom. His cell phone signaled an incoming call. Luckily for him, his place was small. He made it down the hallway to the phone before it went to voice mail.

"Morales."

"Deputy Morales, it's Lesley Robinson."

"Yes?"

"Am I catching you at a bad time?"

"No. It's fine."

"I'd like to set up a meeting for you with the foundation's board. But there are a few things we should go over first. When can we meet?"

"How about now? Do you like Mexican food?"

"Oh, uh, yes, actually, I do, but—"

"You know Señor Tequilas on Collier Boulevard? Why don't you meet me there in half an hour?"

"I'm not...I don't..."

"You have other plans?"

"No."

"I'm starving. You like Mexican food. You want to talk to me. So I'll see you there."

****

Niko waited on the sidewalk in front of the restaurant. He hadn't been raised to be a gentleman, but he'd learned to behave like one. When he'd escaped Jacksonville after Carlos's trial, he had one goal: to leave his past behind. He reinvented himself and became a law-abiding citizen instead of a hoodlum. The DA in Jacksonville helped by greasing the wheels to get

Niko a job in the Waldon County jail, which eventually landed him a spot as a deputy. Niko spent much of his free time filling in the gaps in his education. Courtesy of the public library, he learned proper etiquette, how to dress appropriately, how to survive in the world he aspired to be part of.

Lesley drove into the parking lot in a white Lexus, parking decisively in the first open space she saw. She left the vehicle without checking her makeup in the rearview mirror or fussing with her hair. That she didn't do those things pleased him. Maybe she knew she was stunning and didn't need to reassure herself every five minutes. He liked her no-nonsense attitude.

She wore white slacks and a sleeveless red turtleneck. Her hair wasn't as tightly coiled as the first time they'd met, but she wore it clipped up and back, leaving a sweep of bang to fall across one side. She pushed her sunglasses up on her head as she approached.

He liked the way she looked. Like cool vanilla ice cream with a sweet cherry on top. Too bad she seemed insistent on keeping herself in the back of the freezer. Everything about her said, "Look, but don't you dare touch." Idly Niko wondered what it would take to thaw her, even while he told himself there was no point in trying. His instinct told him she'd be worth the effort.

She gave him a small, polite smile. "Deputy Morales."

"Miss Robinson." He mimicked her tone and smile.

She laughed, throaty and genuine. "All right, you win, Niko. You can call me Lesley if you'd like."

"I'd like. Shall we?" He held the door for her.

The moment they stepped inside a short, round,

dark-haired woman bustled forward. "Ah, Niko, my bambino. Where have you been? I no see you for a week." She pulled him into her embrace, rising on tiptoe to kiss him on both cheeks.

"It's good to see you, too, Alicia," he told her when she stepped back. "This is my friend, Lesley. Lesley, this is Alicia Sanchez. She and her husband Estaban are the owners."

"Nice to meet you," Lesley said.

"Come, come. I have table for you outside, yes?"

"Is that okay?" Niko asked Lesley.

"Sure."

Within minutes they were seated at one of the outside tables. A basket of warm tortilla chips and homemade salsa arrived along with cold bottles of Dos Equis. Niko tapped the neck of his beer bottle against Lesley's. "To beneficial partnerships."

She raised an eyebrow and took a drink straight from the bottle.

"I gotta say I didn't figure you for a beer drinker," said Niko. "The sangria's pretty good here. They're also known for their margaritas."

"Beer with tortilla chips and salsa is one of life's true pleasures," Lesley informed him. She loaded a chip and munched.

"Which you don't allow yourself to indulge in very often." The restaurant wasn't too crowded. Niko staved off starvation by eating his own share of chips and salsa.

Lesley took a careful sip of beer. "Why do you say that?" As if to prove him wrong, she loaded another chip with salsa and popped it in her mouth.

"I'm guessing you're expected to be more of a

23

champagne and *foie gras* kind of girl."

He'd surprised her; he could tell by the flare in her eyes, the sharpness of her gaze, the few seconds of hesitation before she answered. "Yes, well, we all have to deal with expectations. The ones we have of ourselves and the ones others place upon us."

"For example, you didn't expect a guy like me to know what *foie gras* was, let alone be able to pronounce it correctly."

She gave him another of those small smiles acknowledging he'd caught her. "I have a feeling, there's a lot about you that might surprise me."

He tapped the neck of his beer bottle against hers again. "Here's to a future filled with pleasant surprises."

Chapter Four

Lesley placed the telephone receiver back in its cradle and contemplated the school of animated fish swimming across her computer screen. She massaged her shoulders with her fingertips, then rotated her head to work out the tension. The weekly conference call with the senior vice presidents, the CFO and a few department heads had drained her. Although she encouraged an open forum and a free exchange of ideas, the final decisions were hers alone. There were those within the company who resented her presence as her father's hand-picked successor. Under her leadership the company had flourished, yet she still a handful of individuals from her father's tenure who believed they could do better.

The computer signaled an incoming email from her father. She opened it and smiled. He always listened in on the conference calls. *Good job*, she read. *You make me proud.* She sat back and allowed herself a moment to absorb the praise. Every day Richard sent her a brief, encouraging message like this. Sometimes two. He seemed to sense when she was most challenged or stressed, or on the verge of second-guessing her decisions.

A tap on the door interrupted her attempt to reach even the slightest Zen-like state.

"Come in."

Lita slid into the room and closed the door. Lesley thought she saw apology mixed with annoyance and sympathy in her expression.

Lesley's shoulder muscles, which were barely relaxed, tensed all over again. "What is it, Lita?"

"Maria."

For a split second the connection was lost. She put her business face back on. "What about her?"

"She's here."

"Here?"

Lita hesitated.

"*Here*?"

Lita nodded and inclined her head in the direction of the front entrance.

"What does she want?"

"She asked to see your father."

Lesley's brow furrowed. As far as she knew, Maria Delgado's contact with Richard Robinson had been minimal. "Did she say why?"

"No, ma'am. When I told her he was unavailable, she asked to see you. When I told her you were on a conference call, she said she'd wait. I thought under the circumstances..." Lita's voice trailed away.

Lesley glanced at the digital clock on her desk. She'd hoped to have a bit of a breather between the conference call and Ricky's soccer game. She fully expected to be bored to tears, but Ricky asked so little of her and she gave so little of herself she couldn't disappoint him..

She'd get rid of Maria quickly. "It's fine, Lita. Tell her I can give her five minutes."

Lita left and returned, showing Maria in.

"Maria." Lesley kept her tone neutral, merely

26

acknowledging her visitor's presence, and gestured to one of the chairs in front of her desk.

Maria sat, leaning over to place an oversize handbag on the floor. This was not the quiet, mousy servant Lesley remembered, having considered the woman timid and demure. But Maria allowed Steven to seduce her and possessed enough gumption to beg Lesley to raise her child. So perhaps this new version wasn't so far off the mark.

Maria straightened and regarded Lesley with a tentative smile. She'd pushed knock-off designer sunglasses up into her hair. Her bright top featured multicolored flowers and a pair of snug hot-pink capri pants hugged her curves. She also wore makeup, and her hair cascaded around her in a swath of thick, wavy curls. Her artificial nails were painted the same bright pink as her pants.

Lesley also remembered Maria as thin to the point of being malnourished. Now a ripe, curvy vitality oozed from the woman sitting across from her.

Lesley waited. She'd learned this tactic from her father. The first to speak in any negotiation almost always lost. But why did she expect a potential negotiation with Maria? Maria had been shipped out of the country, as far as Lesley knew, over six years ago. Now she was back. This could only mean one thing: she wanted something.

She took up a defensive stance the moment Lita announced Maria's presence. Aware of her rude behavior, she nevertheless drummed her fingers on the edge of her desk while she continued to take in details of Maria's appearance. Big hoop earrings. A cross on a chain around her neck. And a shrewdness in Maria's eyes, a calculating hunger that either hadn't existed or she kept hidden when she worked for the family.

Lesley did a quick reassessment of the events surrounding Maria then. Was it possible she'd been the aggressor in the relationship as Steven claimed? That she wasn't as innocent as Lesley previously believed? Maybe she'd had an agenda even then, believing she'd...what? Be given a permanent place in the household because Lesley's husband fathered her child? Was that why she wanted to see Lesley's father now?

Lesley couldn't hide her annoyance. She glanced again at the digital clock, mentally giving the woman one more minute of her time. If Maria didn't state her business, Lesley would show her the door.

"I want to see Mr. Robinson," she said abruptly, as if she'd read Lesley's mind.

"That won't be possible."

"Five minutes is all I ask."

Intrigued, Lesley tilted her head to one side and studied Maria. "Why?"

"Is between him and me. Five minutes. Then I will know."

"Know what?"

"Please." Her gaze darted about the room. Perhaps she remembered the last time she had asked Lesley for something. "Five minutes and then I go away. You not see me again."

"As appealing as that is, Maria, it isn't possible for you to see my father. He's been ill for quite some time. Six years, in fact. He doesn't receive visitors."

"He is here, no?"

"Where he is, is absolutely none of your business. If you want to tell me what this is about, I may be able to communicate with him. Otherwise, I have another appointment."

"I want to see Ricardo."

The change in tactics came as no surprise. Of course this would have to do with Ricky. Why else would Maria be here? Perhaps she planned to petition Richard for intervention on her behalf. "No."

"He's my son—"

"No. You begged me to take him. If he's anyone's son, he's mine."

"I had no choice—"

"Of course you did. Long before Ricky was born. You chose to sneak around behind my back, sleep with my husband, ignore birth control. You made your choices, Maria. We're all living with them." Lesley stood. "I'll see you out."

"No."

When Maria made no move to rise, Lesley wondered what she'd have to do to get rid of this woman. She made a mental note to talk to Lita about the possibility of hiring a guard of some sort. Except for Ricky and her father, they were a house full of women, unarmed against any physical threat. Although the property was gated, the gates weren't always kept closed during the day when deliveries and service people were expected. Obviously, Maria had an easy time gaining access.

The very last thing Lesley wanted to do was call the cops or create an incident. She thought fleetingly of Deputy Niko Morales. Maria's stubbornness would be no match for someone like him.

Lesley softened her tone, squelching her instinct to lash out, something she'd never done before. "Maria, I

29

understand you may have regrets. But you didn't claim Ricky once he'd recovered from the heart surgery. He was still a baby. You were notified when I filed to formally adopt him. You gave up your rights to him. You signed the documents. I don't want you disrupting his life."

"He's my son," Maria insisted. "If I can't have him, I should get something else. I want to see Mr. Robinson."

Here we go. "What is it you think you should get, Maria? Why don't you tell me why you're here?"

"I will explain to Mr. Robinson. No one else."

"We're done here." Lesley moved to the door and opened it. Maria took her time about picking up her purse and rising from her seat. She sauntered toward Lesley.

"I will contact the newspaper. Tell them how you took my son away from me. How you arranged to have me sent back to El Salvador."

"I did no such thing, and you know it," Lesley hissed. She stepped into Maria's personal space until she was nose to nose with her. Maria didn't flinch. "The newspaper won't publish a word of your story without proof and corroboration. You don't honestly think they'll approach someone in my position and who has the kind of influence I have in the community, do you?"

Lesley wanted to believe she could keep the local paper from publishing anything unflattering about her family. But the *Willow Bay Tribune*, like papers all over the country, was hurting financially, and a juicy story about a wealthy local family, even if unproven, would sell papers. Reporters used words like "allegedly" and "according to" all the time to avoid being sued.

Maria lifted one eyebrow as if Lesley had issued a shocking idea as a personal challenge. She smiled knowingly before moving out into the hallway as slow as possible.

Lesley wished she'd positioned herself in front of Maria instead of being forced to follow behind. At the point where the hallway opened into the entry, Maria quickened her steps. Lesley veered to the left to open the front door, but when she turned Maria was halfway up the stairs.

"Maria!" Lesley used her most commanding tone, but Maria neither slowed down nor looked back. Lesley hustled to the stairs. "Lita," she called, hoping the housekeeper heard her. "I need you."

Maria followed the hallway to the master wing and tried the door of what had once been the master bedroom. Lesley knew it would be locked. The suite had been taken over as her father's convalescent area. The twenty-four-hour nursing staff kept to a strict schedule to minimize interruptions to his routine. Thus the locked door.

Maria pounded on the door. "Mr. Robinson." She said something in rapid-fire Spanish Lesley didn't quite catch. Maria stood her ground as Lesley approached with Lita not far behind.

While Lita spoke indignantly to Maria in Spanish, Lesley reassured the nurse on the other side of the door the situation was under control.

After thirty seconds of listening to the two women argue, Lesley broke in. "Tell her she needs to leave right now, or I'll call the cops."

Maria turned to glare at Lesley. Lita didn't bother to translate. She pointed in the direction of the staircase.

"*Vamanos.*"

Lita and Lesley stayed close behind Maria all the way to the foyer. "I don't want to see you again," Lesley told Maria after Lita opened the door.

Maria gave another glare, this one mixed with something Lesley interpreted as pity, and uttered something that sounded like a curse under her breath. From her oversize handbag, Maria withdrew a piece of paper and shoved it at Lesley.

Lita closed the door behind Maria and locked it.

"Lock all the doors and make certain she's gone, then close the gate and keep it closed," Lesley instructed her. "We aren't expecting anyone else today, are we?"

"No, ma'am."

"Good. We'll have to do something about security." Lesley gazed thoughtfully at the double set of heavy oak doors, then at the paper Maria had given her. "I have a feeling Maria will be back."

****

One glance at the clock told Lesley she didn't have time to change. Already late for Ricky's game, she cursed the traffic lights and road construction and slow drivers on the way to his school.

Still rattled from Maria's visit, she could only think how she was letting him down. Again. She'd felt like a fraud insisting to Maria that Ricky was her son, because deep down she knew she wasn't a mother to him. She hadn't wanted the responsibility for the child Maria foisted on her. She hadn't wanted to lose her handsome husband or the life she'd fooled herself into believing she had. In one willful act on Maria's part, Lesley's life changed forever.

She couldn't forgive Maria and she held it against Ricky, innocent though he was. She didn't like this aspect of herself. The older Ricky got, when his resemblance to Steven became even more apparent, the harder it became for Lesley to behave like the mother she was supposed to be. It wasn't Ricky's fault. Intellectually she knew that. Emotionally, she knew she wasn't dealing with it. Perhaps therapy would help. It wasn't the first time she'd considered it. She wouldn't go to anyone local, however. Willow Bay was much too small a town. She'd have to make arrangements elsewhere. Estero Springs or Sarasota, maybe.

Almost sick with apprehension, Lesley forced herself to breathe deeply, to relax her shoulders and neck. A headache formed behind her eyes, and she wished for nothing more than to be alone, running on the beach, forgetting everyone and everything for just an hour or two.

She found a parking spot in the crowded lot and hustled across the pavement in her high heels. She was half an hour late. Her heels sank into the soft grass as she made her way toward the soccer field. Parents and children clustered along the sidelines. She nodded and smiled to a few she knew as she found a place among them to watch.

She stared at the players on the field and tried to spot Ricky. They were all young boys, many with dark hair and similar builds. *He's my son,* she thought. *I should recognize him immediately, be able to pick him out of a crowd in an instant.* That she couldn't saddened and frustrated her.

She found him, finally, standing on the sideline on the other side of the field. He wasn't playing. He'd spotted her, of course, and knew she was late. She waved a hand in greeting and received a halfhearted wave in return. She'd let him down again. That's surely what he thought. For a moment, she wondered if he wouldn't be better off with Maria. Maybe she would know how to mother him since she'd given birth to him.

But no. Maria wanted only money. Why else would she be so insistent about seeing Lesley's father?

A whistle blew, and there was some sort of break in play. The kids split up to join their coaches and other teammates. They drank water from bottles and listened to the coach. Ricky stood a bit apart from the others, she noticed, as if he weren't part of the team or didn't know his place within it.

I don't fit in here either, she wanted to tell him. *So don't feel badly.* Her sleeveless, gray pinstriped dress and high-heeled black pumps, intended for a business setting, were all wrong here at a soccer field. Most of the mothers, many of whom she knew to be trophy wives, were expensively but casually attired. They brought their own lounge chairs and coolers and huddled in their own clusters with their peers. There were other working mothers there, as well as several fathers who'd obviously left their offices to be here. Even so, most of the mothers were smart enough to wear pantsuits and low-heeled shoes. Many of the fathers removed their ties and rolled up their shirtsleeves.

As Lesley glanced around, she noticed someone else who didn't appear to fit in. He spotted her and made his way toward her.

"Deputy Morales?"

He grinned, which made him even more devastatingly handsome. "I thought we agreed on Niko."

"Yes. Yes, we did, I suppose. Niko." His name didn't roll off her tongue easily. She felt thrown for a loop just as she had from the first time she'd met him.

"How are you?" he asked as if he truly wanted to know.

"Fine. I'm fine. I'm surprised to see you here."

"I met with Ricky's coach earlier. I'm reaching out to all the schools and coaches about donating used equipment to the Challenge Project. But I also met your—that is, I met Ricky after I left our first meeting. I gave him a couple of pointers. He invited me to his games. I told him if I was off work I'd come. I hope it isn't a problem."

"He invited you? No. No problem." *And you remembered?* That's what Lesley wanted to say. This man, this sheriff's deputy she barely knew, had made enough of a connection with Ricky during one meeting that he'd stayed for the game today simply because Ricky asked him to. Was this a ploy on Niko's part, she wondered. A way of getting to her? Or more likely, getting to the foundation's money?

Could he be that conniving? It would have been easy to do a little research and find out she had a son. But surely Niko hadn't engineered an encounter with Ricky that day. He couldn't have known Ricky would be outside, kicking a soccer ball around on his own at the exact moment Niko left the house.

"Tough day?" Niko asked. He'd been studying her while she'd been thinking her suspicious thoughts. It occurred to her that he was the first person in a very long time who'd asked about her day, who even acted interested or as if he cared. She hadn't realized how much she missed it or needed it until this moment.

"It has been, yes. Thank you for asking."

He turned to look at the field, where the players were returning. "Nothing like a kid to take your mind off things, is there?"

"No," Lesley replied thoughtfully. "I suppose there isn't."

Maybe that's what she needed to do. Take the focus off herself, her work, her responsibilities, her loneliness, and put it on Ricky. Spend more time with him. Find something in common with him, build a relationship with him instead of going through the motions, pretending to be his parent when her heart wasn't in it.

Soccer wasn't going to be the common thread she shared with Ricky, she decided. She didn't understand the game. To her it looked like a lot of kids running up and down the field, chasing a ball so they could kick it toward a net. At least Ricky was playing now, although maybe *playing* was too strong a word. He was on the field, although he never got anywhere near the ball.

"What's the score?" she asked Niko. "Is there a score? Do they ever score?"

Niko's chuckle warmed her. She felt some of the tension seep away. "We're up one nil."

"Oh."

Niko Morales didn't do anything she expected him to do. He didn't bring up their meeting or his community center or the foundation. He didn't flirt with her. He watched the game as if he was genuinely interested in the outcome. At one point, when Ricky was as far away from the ball and the other players as he could possibly be, she saw him send a look in Niko's direction. Niko gave him a subtle thumbs-up. Ricky smiled. Lesley remembered Ricky's smile when Niko played with him in the driveway.

She glanced up at the man next to her, wondering how it was possible to feel so comforted by his presence even while inside she tingled with some sort of unfounded anticipation.

"Would you mind if I worked with Ricky?"

"Worked with him?"

"On his soccer." Niko gestured at the field. Ricky was running now, along with a bunch of other kids, trying to block the ball from reaching his team's goal. "He's got good instincts."

Lesley stared at the pack of kids. "He does?"

"He just needs to develop some skill and finesse."

"You can teach him that?"

Niko grinned at her. "I can try."

Something came loose inside Lesley. A chink in her armor fell. She warned herself to retrieve it. Fast. Because just like Steven, a man like Niko Morales could be her undoing. She didn't want to be undone ever again.

"You're not…" She didn't want to say it, but she made herself. She'd know everything she needed to know by his reaction.

Niko's gaze flickered from the field to her and back. "Not what?"

"Doing this to get to me."

He turned his head very slowly and looked at her. She saw the truth in his eyes. She held her breath.

"No." His tone was emphatic, maybe a little

annoyed. Resigned but not angry. He returned his attention to the field.

"You understand why I asked."

"I do."

"But you don't like it."

"No."

"I didn't like having to ask."

"I get that."

Lesley smiled. She understood why Ricky smiled. There was something about Niko Morales, his quiet presence, his interest, that made others want to smile.

"Can I tell you something?" she asked.

Again his gaze flickered from the field to her and back. "Sure."

"I'm bored."

This time he laughed. A genuine, heartfelt laugh that made Lesley want to laugh as well.

The game ended, and after the teams slapped palms, Ricky ran across the field. "Good job, my man," Niko said, offering his fist to Ricky for a bump.

"Did you see it? Did you see my goal?"

"You scored a goal?" Lesley asked.

"Uh-huh. The only one. You missed it. But Niko was here. You saw it, right?"

With an apologetic glance in Lesley's direction, Niko answered. "I did."

"I'm sorry I was late," Lesley said. "Something came up."

"You always say that," Ricky reminded her. "Everybody's going to McDonald's. Can we go?"

Lesley despised fast food, but she wanted to make up for disappointing Ricky. "Sure, if you want."

"Niko can come, too?"

Her gaze met Niko's. "Of course he's welcome to join us, but that's up to him, honey."

Ricky gazed up at him with such a hopeful expression Lesley knew Niko wouldn't turn him down.

"Sure. Thanks."

Ricky jumped up and down in excitement. "Can I ride with you?"

Niko glanced at Lesley. "It's fine," she said. Niko had met him twice and already seemed to have more rapport with the boy than she did. That needed to change.

They headed to the parking lot. Lesley couldn't help but notice a few curious glances sent their way. She knew Willow Bay. Already she could imagine the gossip that would begin again about her, about her possible relationship with Niko. Not to mention Niko's good looks, along with speculation about his sexual prowess. She decided if anyone asked, she'd introduce Niko as a friend and leave it at that.

She arrived at the crowded restaurant before Niko, but was pleased to see he'd installed Ricky in the back seat of his car. She should have expected no less. Niko would know the laws regarding children in cars.

For a moment Lesley considered offering to treat, but she thought better of it.

While they stood in line, a group of boys came in. Lesley remembered one of the reasons why she didn't like places like this. There were always gangs of kids, traveling in packs and sending her radar into overdrive. For some reason she always expected the worst, especially from a group of adolescent males. They were laughing and cutting up with each other as they joined the line behind Lesley.

One of them stepped past Lesley and elbowed Niko's arm. "Hey, Niko, my man."

"Carp! What's up?" Niko seemed genuinely happy to see the kid. He turned to greet the others. "Hey, you guys." They all greeted him in return.

"We got coupons for free Happy Meals," the kid he'd called Carp informed him. "Some lady came and gave a talk in Junior Achievement and handed 'em out."

The cashier handed Niko his order. "We still on for Saturday?"

"Yeah, man. See you there."

Lesley ordered a meal for Ricky and a diet soda for herself. Niko opted for a grilled chicken sandwich and iced tea.

"Would Ricky like to sit with Eric and couple of the other kids?" one of the trophy wives asked Lesley. "We haven't formally met. I'm Christa Bennett."

"Lesley Robinson."

Christa pushed back waves of long blond hair with her left hand so the several bracelets she wore clinked against each other and her hefty diamond ring caught the light. "They have a table together over there." Christa indicated a table for six, where five of the boys were already seated. Two of the mothers hovered over the group, doling out napkins and tiny cups of ketchup.

"Ricky, do you want to sit with the other boys?"

"Okay."

Lesley handed him his meal and his drink. Niko signaled her from a table for two he'd commandeered. "We'll be right over there," she told Ricky.

Lesley tried to shake off her apprehension as she watched Ricky take the last remaining seat. No matter what she did where Ricky was concerned, she was sure it was wrong. She had no maternal instinct to guide her. She thought she'd done the right thing adopting him, but she'd second-guessed herself ever since. Was Ricky better off with her? Should she have sent him to Maria once he was well enough to travel?

She shook her head, wishing she could let go of her insecurity about the decisions she'd made and couldn't change.

By the time she reached the table, Niko had unwrapped his sandwich but hadn't started eating. He was waiting for her. A former gang member with impeccable manners surprised her.

She slid into the seat across from him and set her drink on the table. "Please." She indicated his sandwich. "Go ahead and eat."

"That's all you're having?"

She wrinkled her nose. "You'll think I'm a snob. I don't care for fast food."

"You'll think I'm one too, then, because neither do I. But I'm hungry." He bit into his sandwich. His gaze wandered around the restaurant. From his vantage point he could see Ricky. Lesley's back was to the kids' table.

"Thank you for coming today. I think it meant a lot to Ricky."

His gaze swung back to her. "You should have seen him after he scored that goal. I don't think I've ever seen a kid so excited about anything. Oh, sorry."

"No, it's all right. I wish I'd been there. I intended to, but an unexpected visitor showed up and I couldn't get rid of…although that's no excuse."

Niko's gaze shifted away from her, and he

frowned. Lesley glanced over her shoulder, certain he was watching the table of boys. "What's wrong?"

"Is Ricky having trouble in school?"

"What do you mean? No, not as far as I know. He's in first grade. How much trouble can he have?"

"I mean socially. Does he get along with the other kids? Does he have friends?"

Lesley's face clouded. She glanced again at the boys' table. Ricky's shoulders were hunched. He stared at the food in front of him instead of eating it. Something ugly and painful welled up inside of her. Her own sense of failure swamped her. He was so young, but already there were hints that he wasn't welcome in the circle of kids he went to school with. A birthday party or two she'd heard about after the fact, to which he hadn't been invited. None of the other mothers called to arrange play dates. Ricky didn't belong. He was an outcast because she'd made him one.

She didn't know how to explain any of this to Niko, but before she could try, he bolted from the table. In a second, he was next to the boys' table. The kid Niko had greeted earlier was already there. Ricky was on the floor, his food and drink spilled around him. Carp helped him up. Carp's friends gathered around Ricky like a silent army. Lesley skidded to a halt next to her son, nearly losing her balance in a puddle of soda. "What happened? Are you all right?"

Niko curled his fingers around the upper arm of the boy who occupied the seat next to Ricky's. He pulled the kid to his feet. Silence fell. The other kids at the table were saucer-eyed.

"Get your hands off my son," bellowed a man wading through the crowded tables.

Niko released the boy. "He needs to apologize. Then he needs to clean up the mess he made."

"Who do you think you are?" the man sputtered. "Don't tell me what my son needs to do."

Lesley recognized the boy's father. Irwin Chapman, a local businessman who'd made his fortune in cement. Mitzi was friendly with his first wife, whom he had divorced. After acquiring a younger, dumber wife, he started a second family. This was the result.

"He pushed Ricky off his chair and his meal off the table. I saw it. So did these boys." Niko looked at the four boys still seated. "Didn't you, guys?"

Almost as one, they nodded. Their parents now crowded around.

"So did we," Carp said. His comrades nodded in unison.

Niko stared at Irwin Chapman. "Sir?"

Irwin gave Niko a mutinous glare. He grabbed his son by the arm and hauled him through the mess on the floor. Lesley stepped out of the way with Ricky just in time to avoid being splashed. Irwin glanced back once, fixing his gaze on Niko. "I won't forget this," he said in a threatening tone.

"Neither will I," Niko replied softly.

A yellow bucket appeared, accompanied by a mop-wielding employee who seemed unsurprised and unconcerned with the mess on the floor and quickly cleaned it up, setting a "Caution Wet Floor" cone out as he did.

The parents were murmuring to their sons and to each other. A few of them made sympathetic overtures to Niko and Lesley. Lesley swiped at Ricky's sodden uniform with a wad of napkins. "I'm so sorry," she whispered. He looked at her with tear-filled eyes but said nothing.

"Thanks, guys," Niko said to Carp and his friends. "We'll be okay. Come on, buddy, let's hit the restroom." Niko offered his hand to Ricky and the boy took it. "We won't be long," he told Lesley. "I'll meet you back at the table."

She pushed her soda away and stared at Niko's half-eaten sandwich. Her stomach tied itself in knots. The image of Ricky, humiliated, his shoulders hunched, tears filling his eyes but not falling, wouldn't go away.

"You okay?"

Lesley looked up to find Christa gazing at her.

"I'm fine," she said, forcing a smile. "A little shaken up, I guess."

"Zachary Chapman is a bully, and everyone knows it. Irwin lets him do whatever he wants."

Lesley didn't know how to reply so she said nothing.

"Is there anything I can do?" Christa asked. Lesley decided she was a nice person. She seemed genuine in a way so many of the other parents were not.

"No, but thank you for offering. Niko, er, Deputy Morales took Ricky to the restroom. I'm sure he'll be fine."

"He seems like a nice guy. Deputy Morales, that is. Plus, I couldn't help but notice, he's pretty hot." Christa's giggle made Lesley smile. "If you ever want to get together, for lunch or drinks or something, give me a call."

"I will. Thank you."

"I better go. If I'm not there when Don gets home, I'm in trouble. Bye."

Lesley watched Christa collect her son and bid the other mothers good-bye. She wondered what Christa's life was like. Leisurely, Lesley supposed, if she only had one child. She probably didn't work. But maybe she worked full-time on her marriage to Don, whoever he was.

When Niko and Ricky approached the table, Ricky's clothes were almost dry and he was beaming. Niko evidently worked a miracle while in the restroom.

"Ready to go?" Niko asked abruptly.

"Don't you want to finish eating?"

"I lost my appetite." He gathered up his food and his drink and dropped them in the trash on the way out. Lesley discarded her drink as well.

"Listen," Niko said when they reached Lesley's car. She opened the back door for Ricky. He climbed in and buckled his seat belt. "I told Ricky I'd ask you about taking him to Cambier Park on Saturday for some soccer practice. I've been working with Carp and those other kids who were in there, too."

Lesley didn't know why she hesitated. She trusted Niko even though she barely knew him and met him on only two occasions before today. She'd revised her opinion of Carp and his friends the moment she'd seen them come to Ricky's defense. "I can bring him. What time?"

"Around two?"

"I'll see you then."

"Bye, Ricky," Niko said.

"Bye, Niko."

Lesley gave him a wave and got into her car. Niko waited until she'd backed out and driven away.

****

That night Lesley waited in nervous anticipation for Ricky to finish his bath. She'd asked Lita to let her know when Ricky was ready for bed. In the meantime, she'd gone over and over the events of the day while pacing her room. After her run, she'd showered and changed into a pair of lightweight cotton yoga pants and a short-sleeved hoodie.

It was hard to see Maria as a genuine threat, but Lesley had learned never to underestimate her opponents. Not in business and not in her personal life. She'd noticed a shrewdness behind Maria's eyes, a calculating look that Lesley hadn't seen six years ago. Maria seemed to view herself as the wronged party, when the truth was Lesley did everything she could to help her, including adopting her child.

But you haven't been much of a mother to him, have you? her conscience chided her.

But she was going to change that. Starting tonight. If Ricky would let her.

Lita tapped on her open door. "He's in bed."

"Thanks, Lita."

At Ricky's partially closed door, she knocked softly and stepped in. He sat up in bed with pillows tucked behind his back. The light on his nightstand was on and he was looking at a picture book of dump trucks and earth-moving equipment. He watched her approach, his expression neutral. She swore she caught wariness in his eyes and wondered what caused it.

Lesley sat on the edge of the bed and licked her dry lips. She'd rehearsed a bit of a speech in her head earlier but couldn't remember a word of it. "I'm not a very good mother, am I?" She tried to smile, but failed.

"You're not my mother," Ricky said. It wasn't

meant as an insult. Lesley'd seen no reason to pretend with him. He knew he was adopted. "I don't have a mother. Or a father."

He looked down at his book and fiddled with the pages.

"The truth is, Ricky, you do have a mother." His head came up. "You have two, the one who gave birth to you and me, because I adopted you when she couldn't take care of you."

Lesley hesitated, unsure where to go now that she'd started. "The thing is, I don't think I'm so good at taking care of you, either."

"Are you going to give me away, too?"

"No. No. Nothing like that. When a mother has a baby, usually she naturally knows how to take care of it. If she's able to, that is. Yours couldn't, so I said I would, but I wasn't prepared. I didn't know how. I was scared, I guess."

"Grownups don't get scared."

Lesley smiled. "It seems that way, doesn't it? But they do. They're probably scared of more things than kids are, because they know more about what can hurt them."

Ricky frowned as if he didn't quite believe her.

"Maybe I can explain it better sometime. But for right now, what I wanted to say is I'm going to try harder to be a better mother to you."

"Like come to my soccer games? And not be late?"

"Yes. Like that." She paused for a moment. "You know, Ricky, a lot of things happened when you were born. That's when Grandpa got sick. We were all worried about him and about you, too. There was a lot for me to do."

47

"Like run Grandpa's company?"

"Exactly. All of a sudden I became the boss at work because Grandpa couldn't be. I guess I kind of turned into the boss at home, too. I was so busy being the boss, I never learned how to be a mother."

"You can be a bossy mother. I won't mind."

"I'd like to be just your mother, if that's okay with you."

Ricky beamed. "Sure. Can I call you Mom instead of Lesley?"

"I think I'd like that."

"Maybe if I call you Mom, you'll get better at being one."

"Maybe. I'm sorry, Ricky. That's what I wanted to say. I'm sorry, and I'll try harder. You might have to tell me what you need because I won't always know. You'll have to train me, okay?"

"Like how Niko is going to train me to play soccer?"

"Something like that."

"Okay."

Lesley smiled and patted his knee through the covers. Kids were so much more accepting than adults.

"You should hug me now," Ricky informed her. "I'm pretty sure that's what moms do."

"Okay." She leaned forward. Ricky put his arms around her neck and squeezed tight. She held him close and squeezed him back. She waited for him to break the embrace, but it was a long time coming. He was probably making up for all the bedtime hugs he'd missed from her in the last six years.

Finally he let go and settled himself back on the pillows. "You hug pretty good," he told her. "Maybe if you practice you can get better at it."

Lesley smiled at Ricky's adult tone, repeating words he'd heard her or others say. "We can try again tomorrow, okay? Goodnight." Lesley stood and turned his light off. She bent down and kissed the top of his head.

"Night, Mom."

Chapter Five

Niko didn't know a whole lot about soccer. He hoped no one discovered his secret. Most of what he knew he remembered from his early years, when he'd played in elementary school. He watched it on TV a few times, and since moving to Willow Bay he'd volunteered as an assistant coach for a league in which a couple of the other deputies coached teams for their kids.

He'd studied training videos on YouTube and borrowed *Soccer for Dummies* at the library. He figured he knew enough about the basics and the rules to get by. Besides, this was about more than developing their soccer skills. It had to do with building a rapport with them, boosting their self-confidence and teaching them to get along with each other.

Three other boys came this Saturday. They were older than Ricky Robinson, but he'd worked with them before. They were good kids who struggled in middle school and had minor brushes with the law. Statistically they were considered "at risk."

He'd located them through a couple of different agencies. These were the kind of kids his community center would be all about. He'd been up front about his intentions with the kids and with their mothers. They were part of his experiment, to see if the path they were on could be changed if he intervened early enough.

He and the boys arrived early to kick the ball around. The kids tried out some fancy moves they'd worked out on their own, trying to impress and outdo each other. As long as they kept it friendly, Niko let them.

From behind his sunglasses he tracked Lesley's approach with Ricky, trudging along beside her, carrying his soccer ball. Lesley wore a simple dress, flat sandals and no jewelry except for a tank watch and gold hoop earrings. Her hair was clipped back as usual, but the slight breeze blew a few strands around her face.

She pushed her sunglasses into her hair and greeted him. After he acknowledged her, he hunkered next to Ricky. "How you doin', pal? Ready for a workout?"

Ricky nodded vigorously.

"Hey, guys," Niko called. He signaled them over and introduced everyone. "Why don't you show Ricky what you've been working on? I'll be over in a minute."

The older boys did as they were told. Lesley watched in apprehension at first but soon relaxed. The boys didn't seem to mind that Ricky was half their age. They made him part of their group.

Niko followed her gaze but turned back to her as he spoke. "They're good kids. You don't have to worry."

"I can see that."

****

Lesley lowered her sunglasses and focused on him from behind the dark lenses. He wore a gray T-shirt with the sheriff's department logo on the breast pocket, running shorts, and sneakers. Everything she saw she liked. He was in good shape, his forearms and calves roped with muscle.

"I wanted to ask you something," she said.

He waited.

"Would you happen to know anyone…that is, I think I need to hire someone, preferably male, to provide household security for us."

Niko went on alert. "Is there a problem? A specific threat?"

"No. Not exactly. There was an incident the other day that made me think it would be a good idea to have someone on the premises round-the-clock. Someone who could fit into the setting, our routine. But I'd prefer not to use a professional agency. I don't want someone in uniform, someone not in my own employ. I thought a retired cop, perhaps?"

"I might know someone. He retired a couple of years ago. I haven't seen him lately, but he might be interested. If he is, I'll have him call you. His name's Mitch Hayes."

Lesley breathed a sigh of relief. "Thank you. I appreciate it."

Even with sunglasses shading their eyes, Lesley sensed something going on between them. Some kind of undercurrent she couldn't quite get a handle on. "I should go."

"You're welcome to stay."

She gazed at the kids running across the grass. "I have a few errands, but maybe I'll come back early and bring snacks and drinks for the boys. What do you think?"

"They won't turn it down, that's for sure."

She gave him an affirmative nod and a slight smile. "I'll do that, then."

****

He watched her walk across the park to her car, all the while reminding himself there was no use developing an interest in a woman so far out of his reach. Didn't mean he couldn't dream, though.

For an hour, Niko coached the boys through drills. Afterward he let them make up their own games as part of the practice, using the soccer ball. He wanted them to learn, but also to have fun and to get to know each other better. Carp, whose given name was Carpenter Mosley, was a born leader. He was smart, well-mannered, and charming, but without strong guidance, Niko feared he could easily be seduced into making some poor decisions. His mother was a nurse. She did her best to set a good example and monitor Carp's friends and activities. But Niko was convinced these kids needed more.

Part of the center's goal was to find mentors for the at-risk kids. He envisioned softball games, fishing trips, maybe even golf outings to mix the mentors with the boys. A barbecue. A Ping-Pong tournament. Niko had no shortage of ideas. All he needed was funding, volunteers, and time.

When the kids took a break, Niko handed out bottles of water.

"I have to go to the bathroom," Ricky told him.

"Carp? You want to take Ricky to the restroom? Anybody else need to go?"

No one else did, but Carp seemed pleased to have been selected as bathroom escort. He headed off with Ricky, shortening his stride so the boy could keep up. Niko watched, feeling an odd sort of pride in them. The concrete-block restroom wasn't too far away, and he trusted Carp to keep an eye on Ricky. He turned his attention back to the other two boys.

Five minutes later, when Carp and Ricky hadn't returned, Niko looked back to the restrooms. The two boys were talking to a woman. Or more accurately, the woman was speaking to Ricky while Carp stood patiently next to him with his arms across his chest.

Something about the scene seemed off to Niko, but he couldn't put his finger on what. The woman looked to be Latina. She had lots of dark hair and wore bright colors. Big sunglasses obscured her features. She carried a bulging, oversize purse.

"You guys stay here," he said to the other two boys.

He stalked toward the restrooms, his gaze fixed on the woman. She must have sensed his approach or Carp must have shifted his attention to him because Niko thought she glanced his way although she'd hardly moved her head. She said something else to Ricky, patted his shoulder, and took off at a trot toward the playground. She strode past the fenced area, along the narrow walkway separating the tennis courts, and disappeared from view.

"Who was that?"

Carp shrugged.

"Do you know her?" Niko asked Ricky.

"No, sir."

"What did she want?" Niko asked more harshly than he intended.

Ricky took a tiny step away from him and closer to Carp. Niko told himself to calm down, but a thousand scenarios flashed through his head as he hustled toward the restrooms. Ricky Robinson belonged to a wealthy, prominent family. Lesley had mentioned her security concerns. Ricky would be an excellent target for a kidnapper. He was a loner. He'd been playing outside on the estate grounds the first time Niko met him. The gates were wide open. Anyone could walk in and snatch the kid. Was this woman doing recon? Had Ricky almost been a target? On Niko's watch?

He lowered himself to Ricky's level. "Sorry. Let's walk back." He reached for Ricky's hand and the boy took it. "What did she want?" he asked more gently. "It looked like you were having quite the conversation."

"She asked about soccer and if you were a coach. How old am I and what school am I in."

"She said she had a little boy the same age as Ricky," Carp added. "She just moved here and she wanted him to meet other kids."

"Did she ask where you live?"

"No," Ricky said.

"How about your name?"

"Yes."

"Did you tell her?"

"Yes."

They reached the other two boys, and Niko indicated to Ricky and Carp to take seats. Once his heart rate returned to normal and every unpleasant scene he'd just imagined had been put back in its place, he decided to use the incident as a teachable moment to talk to the boys about stranger danger.

****

The following evening when her cell phone rang, Lesley almost ignored it. She was running a bath. After learning of an explosion in one of their plants in Honduras, her stress level zoomed off the charts. She'd monitored reports, participated in several conference calls, and directed her media relations department to execute a response. Luckily there were only minor injuries and minimal damage.

She glanced at the local number she didn't recognize, and hesitated before she answered.

"Lesley? It's Niko Morales."

As if he needed to identify himself beyond his first name, Lesley thought, and smiled. Still, she liked the formality he used. Very attractive. "Niko. How are you?"

"Well, thank you. And you?"

"Well, also, thank you for asking." Since he couldn't see her, she didn't bother to hide her smile.

"I talked to Mitch Hayes. He's interested in meeting with you about providing security. I have his number."

"Oh. All right. Hold on just a moment…Go ahead." She tapped the number into her phone and read it back to Niko. She wished she could think of some reason to keep him on the line. She liked the sound of his voice. She liked the way he asked after her well-being. Even if he was just being polite, she wanted to believe he was truly interested. She squashed the thought immediately and made herself say, "Thank you. If that's all then?"

"Actually, no. I didn't want to mention this in front of Ricky yesterday, but maybe he told you about the woman who approached him at the park."

"No. He didn't."

"It was probably nothing," Niko said. "Carp took Ricky to the restroom. When they came out, this woman started chatting Ricky up."

"Describe her."

"Latina. Early twenties. Five-four, one-twenty. Long dark hair. Big purse. Big sunglasses." When Lesley said nothing, Niko went on. "I got a little spooked, I guess. You were looking for a security guard. Ricky said he didn't know her. She took off as soon as she saw me coming. I thought you should know."

"Thank you for telling me."

"Anything I can do to help?"

Lesley didn't know how to answer that. She almost couldn't comprehend Maria's nerve. "I don't think so."

"All right then. Good night," Niko said after a moment. She wondered if she imagined a note of coolness in his tone.

"Good-bye." Lesley clicked off and stepped into the oversize tub.

She sank down into the pulses of warm water generated by the jets. Fragrant bubbles covered the surface, and she closed her eyes as she leaned her head back against the rim of the tub. She forced herself to relax, concentrating on each part of her body, starting with her toes and working her way up. She used the deep breathing she'd learned from yoga to let most of the tension of the day seep out of her.

If Maria's boldness continued, Lesley would definitely have to step up security arrangements. She wasn't taking any chances with her father or her son. Or anyone else in her household. Maybe all Maria wanted was to see Ricky, see how he was doing. She hoped so. But somehow she doubted it.

She reminded herself why she needed to keep everyone at arm's length. Business was business. She didn't get attached, and she didn't get personally involved. She insulated herself because otherwise— otherwise she was afraid she'd fall apart. If she fell apart, so would everything else in her world. It wasn't just her world, though. It was her parents, Ricky, Lita. The business built by her father she kept going. The foundation. Everyone who relied on her. Everyone she couldn't afford to let down.

How Niko Morales ducked under her radar mystified her. She couldn't quite fathom how he'd managed to establish a relationship with her son and with her so quickly. From the moment she'd met him, she'd trusted him, but she questioned her own judgment. He was a former gang member and led a life far different from hers. Why should he inspire trust?

She couldn't answer that question. She saw how Ricky responded to him, how she herself responded to him, although she tried to hold herself back. Somehow they'd created a rapport. He'd rescued Ricky, and now he was potentially rescuing her and her family, assuming Mitch Hayes took the job.

Thinking about Niko made her tense up again in an entirely different way, and she told herself to stop. She gave herself ten minutes of breathing and relaxation techniques before she adjusted her position. She dried her hands on the towel she'd placed nearby and reached for her paperback novel. Lesley stared at the cover, which depicted a beautiful young woman baring an abundance of cleavage, golden tresses falling down her back, who was about to be ravaged by a dark-haired, bare-chested, steel-abbed hero in a kilt.

Lesley stuck her fingers into the fat bag of chocolate-covered peanuts next to the towel and briefly contemplated one before she popped it in her mouth. She settled back in the warm water, sighed, and opened her book.

****

Physically, Mitch Hayes wasn't what Lesley expected. He was of average height and medium build. But he carried himself like a military man, shaking hands like he meant business, and when he spoke, his voice held a note of authority.

"I understand you have a security problem." He said it as if he were the one conducting the interview.

Lesley hesitated, disarmed by his directness. "I wouldn't say it's a problem, but there was an incident a few days ago that made me think I'd like to have someone on premises better able to deal with a physical threat than Lita and I were."

"A physical threat? Care to elaborate?"

"A former member of the household staff arrived unannounced. She wanted to see my father, who is unable to receive visitors."

"Why is that?"

"He suffered a debilitating stroke several years ago. He has round-the-clock care, but he rarely receives visitors outside the family and doesn't leave his suite."

At Mitch's nod, Lesley continued. "I met with this...individual and explained the situation. As I was escorting her out, she ran upstairs before I could stop her. I called for Lita, and we managed to convince her it was in her best interests to leave. She did, but I'm...uncomfortable with our current security arrangements."

"Which are?"

Lesley outlined them.

"You have a lot of coming and going through your gate," Mitch commented.

Lesley nodded. "Which is why it's often left open during the day. Normally, if it's closed, Lita authorizes access. But she isn't always here, nor is my mother."

"This former employee," Mitch said, "did she say why she wanted to see your father?"

"She wouldn't tell me."

"Did they have a history of some sort?"

"None. My father was still active when she worked here, but he traveled often and any interaction between them would have been limited. She was technically employed by my former husband and myself."

Mitch raised an eyebrow. "That's a pretty gutsy move on her part, going upstairs without your authorization or invitation."

"I agree."

"It sounds like an act of desperation."

"It may very well have been. At any rate, I'm looking for someone who can fit into the household. I'd like it if you could drive my son to and from school. Perhaps relieve Lita of some of the household responsibilities where appropriate. You'd have use of the guest house. If you're interested in the job, of course."

"I might be."

Lesley tried not to let her relief show. She'd decided Mitch was the ideal candidate for the job, but she couldn't believe her search for someone to fill the position would be so easy. "Let me show you the house and grounds and introduce you to Lita."

Lesley concluded the guided tour in the driveway next to Mitch's SUV. It was the kind of capable-looking vehicle she'd expected him to have, and she could see it was well maintained. She bet he kept the gas tank full as well. The longer she spent in his company, the more she liked him. He'd asked a few questions about the household routine, seemed satisfied with the living quarters, and made brief small talk with Lita.

The front door opened, and Mitzi stepped out, dressed for lunch at the club. "There you are, darling," she trilled as she came down the steps.

"Mother, I'd like you to meet Mitch Hayes. Mitch, my mother, Mitzi."

There was a clasping of hands between the two of them, but Lesley wasn't sure who instigated it. Mitch surely, for her mother's impeccable manners would have prevented her from offering to shake hands with a man upon introduction. Far from the businesslike handshake Mitch exchanged with Lesley, however, this was more of a prolonged squeeze neither seemed inclined to end.

Odd, Lesley thought as she gazed from her mother to Mitch and back.

"Pleased to meet you," her mother said breathlessly, her gaze never leaving Mitch's face.

"Likewise, I'm sure," Mitch replied. He seemed just as entranced with Mitzi as she was with him.

Her mother was an attractive woman. Mitzi spent an inordinate amount of time and money aging as gracefully as possible, stopping just shy of cosmetic surgery. As a result she looked damn good for a woman who'd lived over half a century.

As if Mitzi suddenly became aware of her inappropriate behavior, she relinquished her hold on

Mitch's fingers and adjusted the fit of her jacket at the waist. "Well. I'm off to lunch," she said, vaguely directing the statement to both of them. Her attention focused back on Mitch. "Lovely to meet you. I hope to see you again."

Mitch grinned, something Lesley hadn't seen him do before. It transformed his face. "Same here," he assured her mother.

She gave a nervous giggle, slid behind the wheel of her car, and waggled her fingers at them. Mitch fired back with a casual two-fingered salute before he turned back to Lesley. "I'll take the job."

Chapter Six

Lesley paced nervously outside the open doors of the boardroom. The foundation's other members were already seated inside. They were elderly, for the most part: retired executives who'd successfully run companies and who now sat on boards like this one, played golf, and traveled. They'd been handpicked by her to sit on the Robinson Family Foundation's review committee. They were tough, fair, and honest. She almost always agreed with their decisions. Normally, she never got personally involved with any of the applicants. Except for Niko Morales.

She turned at the end of the hallway to pace back the way she had come when she saw him approach. She slowed her steps and focused on controlling her reaction to him. She'd seen him in a sports coat, casual slacks, and a polo shirt—and in his deputy's uniform.

But Niko Morales in a dark blue, pinstriped suit and a red power tie nearly took her breath away.

She smiled. "Hello. It's good to see you again."

He grinned. "Likewise." He glanced briefly into the boardroom. "Ready to throw me to the lions? Do I get a net and spear at least?"

Lesley chuckled. "They're not that bad. You'll do fine. I'm certain of it." Suddenly, she was. Niko's quiet presence was sure to impress the review panel. He was confident and genuine and intelligent. Lesley knew he'd be able to answer every question the committee put to him. She was almost certain his grant would be approved.

"Thank you for the vote of confidence. Should we go in?"

****

Niko performed beautifully. The PowerPoint slideshow she'd suggested he create enhanced his presentation. Lesley could tell the committee members were equally impressed with him. "You'll be hearing from us by the end of next week," Lance Langtree said as he shook Niko's hand.

"Thank you, sir. I look forward to your decision."

The others said their goodbyes and filed out, leaving Niko and Lesley alone. "You did great."

Niko loosened his tie and unbuttoned the top button of his crisp white shirt. "You think so? They asked a lot of questions."

"All of which you answered to their satisfaction. They're interested in your project. I can tell."

"You think they'll approve the funding?"

"All I can say for sure is you've got my vote."

"I'd invite you out for a drink to celebrate but—"

"It's a bit premature? When you have three more votes, we can celebrate."

"I'm thinking we should celebrate me getting through today without blowing it." Niko started to walk her out.

"You acted like it was nothing. You didn't seem nervous at all."

"Then I'm a better actor than I thought."

"You weren't acting," Lesley said with certainty.

He pushed open the door to the parking lot.

64

"Where are you parked?"

Lesley pointed. When they reached her vehicle, she paused. "You said you'd invite me out for a drink—but. But what?"

"We don't exactly run in the same circles."

She waited because everything inside her wanted to prolong her time in his company. "True."

"My idea of a drink somewhere is a beer with some wings at a sports bar or nachos at Señor Tequilas. Your idea of a drink is champagne at a country club where they wouldn't hire me to wash the dishes."

"But I always order wings or nachos with my champagne."

Niko studied her for a moment before he seemed to make a decision. "I'm going to stop by Bubba's. It's a sports bar on the North Trail. Best wings in town. You in?"

"I'm in."

****

"There's something I wanted to ask you about," Lesley said once they were seated, cold bottles of beer in front of them, an order of wings on its way. From her purse, she took the piece of paper Maria had given her and handed it to him.

He studied it for a moment. "Who are these people?"

"That's my father," she said, pointing. "I think this might be Maria's mother."

He studied it a moment longer, then handed the paper back. "Who's Maria?"

"If my guess is right, she's the woman you saw talking to Ricky at the park." Lesley turned her bottle of beer around and around on the table, watching the rings of condensation gather beneath it before she looked him in the eye. "She's Ricky's mother."

"I thought you were Ricky's mother."

Lesley winced. "Maria is Ricky's biological mother. She's from El Salvador. I haven't seen her in six years, not since Ricky was born. She showed up out of the blue the day I was late for Ricky's soccer game."

Niko straightened. "What did she want?"

He'd taken off his jacket and tie and left them in the car. He'd rolled up the sleeves on his shirt and loosened the top two buttons. Lesley temporarily got sidetracked staring at his Adam's apple and the hollow of his throat she could see beneath it.

She lifted her gaze back to his. "I'm not sure. She wanted to see my father. I told her no. She said she wanted Ricky, that he was her child. I told her no."

"Is she what made you decide to get a security guard?"

"Yes. Her behavior made me realize we are not prepared for a physical threat. My mother, me, Lita. Ricky and my father? There's always a nurse on the premises as well, but..."

"You're vulnerable."

"Yes. I don't like it. Now, of course, we have Mitch. Thank you for that, by the way."

"It's working out?"

"Yes. My mother and Ricky adore him. He's taken some of the workload off Lita."

"And you can stop worrying."

"Yes."

The wings arrived, and they helped themselves. Eventually Niko said, "You wanted to ask something."

"I did." She cut a bit of chicken off the bone,

dipped it into the bleu cheese dressing, then put it in her mouth to savor. "Yum."

"Wings are a finger food," Niko informed her, picking up one and biting into it.

"I know. But they're so messy." Again Lesley dipped her bite of chicken and popped it into her mouth. After she swallowed, she said, "What difference does it make how I eat them as long as I'm enjoying them?"

"None, I suppose." He wiped his fingers and mouth with a napkin and drank some of his beer.

Lesley contemplated the piece of celery she'd dipped in bleu cheese. "I didn't tell Mitch every detail about my history with Maria."

"You don't trust him?"

"I do. But there are some things about our past history I'd prefer to keep private."

"So the question is does he need to know everything?"

"Yes." Lesley bit into the celery.

"Is your history with Maria going to compromise your safety now, do you think? Or the safety of anyone in your household?"

"I don't know. She knows the house, of course."

"Is Mitch having knowledge of this private information going to make him better able to protect you?"

Lesley weighed the question for a minute before she answered. "I don't see how."

"Do you think she's dangerous? Do you think she wants to cause you or your family harm?"

"Yes, but not the way you mean. I think she wants something from us, from me, perhaps. She might go after Ricky, but I don't think she'd hurt him."

Niko leaned across the table. "Go after him? Do you mean kidnap him?"

Again Lesley considered the question, surprised to realize it was a possibility she hadn't fully considered. "Maybe. I'm not sure."

Niko frowned.

"What is it?"

"That day at the park I should have known Ricky could be in danger. Frankly, he'd be a good target for a kidnapper."

"You're right."

"I gave all the boys the 'stranger danger' speech. Every kid needs to have it drilled into him how easy it is for a predator to lure him into a potentially harmful situation."

"I need to be more vigilant. From now on, I will be."

Niko sat back, picked up his beer. "Mitch needs to know she's a potential threat to you and to Ricky."

"He knows."

"He just doesn't know why."

"Not all of it, no."

"What he'd need is as much information as you have about her now. Where she lives. What she's doing. A phone number. Make and model of her vehicle. A picture of her."

"I don't have any of that. I've only seen her once. She threatened me, threw this at me, and left."

"What did she threaten you with?"

Lesley reached for her beer. "She threatened to expose a private matter. I'd rather not go into details."

"Fair enough." After a pause, he asked, "What's

the connection between Maria's mother and your father?"

"I don't know. Obviously they were acquainted."

"Were they involved?"

Lesley squirmed. "I don't want to think so."

"But you don't know?"

"No."

"Let me see the picture again."

Lesley handed it to him.

He spoke as he studied it. "They aren't posed as if they're lovers. They aren't even touching each other. Your father's hands are clasped together." Niko glanced at Lesley for confirmation. "All this picture proves is that your father and Maria's mother were photographed at the same place at the same time. It doesn't mean anything, does it? It's not proof of anything."

"No, I suppose not."

"It's not even a complete picture. Something's been cut out of it. Hard to tell what since it's a photocopy of what looks like an old newspaper photo." He handed the paper back to her before he spoke again. "The basic rule of thumb is when someone's priority is to protect you, make sure they've got all the information they need to do the job."

Chapter Seven

Steven Lambert wasn't in the habit of welcoming casual visitors to his townhouse. In fact, unless it was a handpicked, overnight visitor of the female persuasion, he rarely had visitors at all. In the past year, since he'd decided to make a bid for the state senate, even those casual overnight visits stopped.

Running for office would be tricky enough given his past difficulties with Lesley and without the Robinson family support. He'd had it all, and he'd thrown it away. All his carefully laid plans were ruined, and there was no one to blame but himself. Deep down he knew this, which is why he never admitted it to anyone. Instead he blamed anyone and everyone else involved. Maria for seducing him. Lesley for throwing him out without a penny. Maria's child for its mere existence.

He'd played Lesley so well for so long, and she'd bought it all. She'd actually believed he hadn't been interested in her for her family's fortune. Of course he'd married her for that, and the connections, and the power he assumed would all be his one day.

He'd pretended to admire his wife's intelligence and ambition, but in truth he'd resented it. He wanted a woman to be in awe of him, for her world to revolve around him. Lesley had loved him, but she'd wanted to create a life for herself as well. She'd wanted them to be life partners. Sharing work and family and children and intertwining it all into their relationship.

Steven didn't know what he expected when he looked through the peephole of his door, but it wasn't Maria. Even that brief glimpse of her sent blood pumping to his cock.

Maria was everything Lesley wasn't. Dark haired, sloe eyed, bronze skinned. He could still recall the feel of her full breasts and her rounded hips and thighs. He had done things to and with Maria he'd never done with another woman before or since. She adored him, stroked his ego as well as his cock, centered her narrow world around him. When Lesley traveled, Maria was there, offering him comfort and understanding along with her body.

But she'd foolishly become pregnant. She'd expected him to leave Lesley and her fortune and marry her. Live in squalor and raise a child with her, and, knowing Maria, she'd expected to have a passel more.

He'd done his best to get rid of her and her unborn child before the shit hit the fan. But the wheels of INS moved slowly even when they'd been greased, and sending Maria packing back to Guatemala or El Salvador or wherever the hell she came from hadn't happened soon enough.

Steven had been in a rage when Maria's sickly baby arrived early, before INS finally made a move to revoke her visa. Heroic, self-sacrificing Lesley rescued the baby and, once she'd learned the truth of it all, kicked Steven to the curb. Maria ruined everything for Steven.

But still, he wouldn't mind fucking her.

He opened the door and got a good look at her. His

first thought was she looked good, if you liked the glitzy, overblown look some Latino women achieved naturally. Just the right amount of bling, the blouse a little too tight, a skirt that hugged all the curves, a sheen of silky dark hair swinging across the shoulders. He stared at her without saying anything. Her tentative smile died on her lips. She stared at him, too, giving him a wary yet bold assessment.

He stepped back then to see what she'd do. She stared at him a moment longer, then sashayed across the threshold, removing the designer sunglasses she'd pushed into her hair and stowing them in her designer bag. Probably both knockoffs.

Steven caught a whiff of her scent, probably another knockoff of some designer perfume. He couldn't help the quick, brief fantasy of shoving her up against the wall and taking her, slaking his lust in her ripe body before showing her the door.

A few years ago he'd have done just that. But he was older now. Wiser. Not prone to make the same mistakes he'd made before. At least not with the same woman.

Lesley was away on a business trip the first time Maria captured his attention. He'd barely noticed the quiet, mousy domestic before that. She hovered at the edges of his existence, cleaning or doing laundry. She had a room wherever the servants were housed on the Robinson estate. He'd barely given their accommodations any thought, and he'd hardly noticed Maria because her work schedule coincided with his. Their paths rarely crossed, and if they did, he'd ignored Maria anyway. He was doing his best to keep Lesley content while he mined her social and business network to further his political ambitions.

But then Lesley flew to Pittsburgh for a board meeting and Maria arrived for work early. He'd registered something different about her then without thinking too much about what it was. Her hairstyle? Her uniform? He'd left for the office only to discover her in the kitchen when he returned that evening.

She'd been putting the finishing touches on a small tray of fruit, cheese, and crackers. He noticed her smile because he'd never seen it before. Was the skirt of her uniform shorter? The neckline of her blouse lower?

She'd greeted him. The tray was for him, since Miss Lesley was away, she explained. He worked so hard, after all. Surely he was hungry after a long day. She offered to pour him a drink if he would like.

So willing. So accommodating. So concerned about him. Not that Lesley hadn't been, but Lesley demanded equal time for her own needs. If she listened to a recount of his day, he had to feign interest in hers.

But Maria hung on his every word, especially after he'd suggested she pour herself a drink and join him. That's how it all started.

A year later, it blew up in his face.

They squared off to face each other now. Steven waited, but when Maria said nothing, he did. "Why are you back?"

"To visit my father."

She set her purse on an end table and plopped herself in the middle of his living room sofa, glancing around at her surroundings. Warily, Steven moved into the room. He crossed his arms over his chest and watched her, wondering what kind of game she was playing. As far as he knew, she'd been raised by a single mother in small village near San Salvador until she'd obtained a work visa and arrived at the Robinsons' to work for him and Lesley.

"Your father," he echoed, not bothering to hide his skepticism.

She stared at him. "Richard Robinson."

Steven guffawed, the shock of her statement causing a full belly laugh to erupt from deep inside him. The suggestion that his business-tycoon former father-in-law had sired this Central American domestic struck him as the funniest thing he'd heard in months.

Maria's full lips thinned. Her eyes narrowed. She waited until he stopped laughing. He swiped at the tears near his eyes. "Good one, Maria. You're even crazier now than you were six years ago."

"I am not loco. I can prove it."

"Really?" Steven shook his head. "I've got to hear this. But first I need a drink."

He poured himself one but didn't offer her anything. He didn't want her to stay and was almost sorry he'd let her in. He'd get rid of her as quickly as possible because, as much as he blamed her for his past mistakes, Maria Delgado did something for him other women failed to do. Maybe it was chemistry or pheromones or his own weakness, but he couldn't afford to get involved with her again.

He slouched into a club chair across from her and took a sip of his bourbon on ice. "So Richard Robinson is your father. Funny, you never mentioned it before."

"I did not know before."

"Ah, well, now it all makes sense."

"I did not know until my mother died."

"Uh-huh." Steven sipped his drink. Maria could

share her delusions with him. He didn't have any other plans for the evening, and at least her arrival was an interesting diversion. Then he'd send her on her way and hope he never saw her again. Belatedly he remembered his manners. "Sorry to hear about your mother."

Maria sniffed. "Did Richard have a scar on his arm? His right arm?"

Steven shrugged. "How should I know?"

"You were married to his daughter. You lived in the same house."

"A scar. On his arm. *That's* how you're going to prove he's your father. All claims to the contrary, if you think that will prove anything, you are crazy."

"I have a picture."

"Of him? With a scar on his arm?" Steven took another sip of his drink. "Why didn't you say so?"

"Part of a picture," Maria amended.

"This gets better and better," Steven murmured more to himself than to her. "Tell you what. Why don't you take your picture and your claim to Lesley? Tell her what you told me. See if she believes you."

"I already saw her."

"Did you now? I guess that didn't go too well or you wouldn't be here."

"She wouldn't let me see him."

Steven barked out a laugh. "Of course not. No one's seen him in six years except his family and his medical staff."

"He is...unwell?"

"Practically a vegetable from what I understand. What did Lesley say when you told her he was your father?"

75

"I didn't tell her. I only asked to see him. I thought if I could see his arm, then I'd know."

Steven felt a twinge of sympathy for Maria he didn't want to feel. She had no idea what she was up against. The Robinson family empire could destroy people like her. He knew what it felt like to be the beneficiary of their generosity, and he knew how it felt to be frozen out of their privileged circle. "Would you like a drink?" he heard himself ask.

Maria gave him a tremulous smile. "Yes, thank you."

He mixed her a vodka and tonic without asking what she wanted. She accepted it graciously and took a delicate sip. His cordiality relaxed her. She settled back into the sofa and crossed her legs. Steven noticed. She wore strappy sandals with fuck-me high heels. Her toenails were painted hot pink. He took another sip of bourbon and brought his attention back to her face.

She was a good actress, he'd give her that. Six years ago she'd played the part of the helpless, naïve girl to the hilt. She'd probably pretended to a virginity that didn't exist and an innocence she'd left behind long ago. But he hadn't been sophisticated enough to see through her then. Now, however, he knew her innocent smile for what it was. She pretended she hadn't noticed his perusal of her crossed legs. She thought she could play on his sympathy, but she was wrong. He'd hear her story and then he'd show her the door.

"I think you can help me."

Steven quelled the impulse to roll his eyes. Maria didn't know he was the one who'd gotten her ousted from the country before. If she did, he'd be the last person she'd ask for help.

"I doubt I can be of any help to you at all, but why don't you tell me what this is all about?" Forewarned was forearmed, after all.

"I did not know who my father was. My mother would not say. But after she died, I found pictures. One is only part of a picture," she amended again. "Of my mother and a man next to her, but it is torn and his face is not visible. Only part of him."

"The arm with the scar."

"Yes, but he is white. The other is a picture of my mother and Richard Robinson."

"Doing what?"

"Nothing. Sitting next to each other."

"How exactly do you think your mother hooked up with a white guy who may or may not be Richard Robinson?"

"She worked in a factory. Sewing for many American companies."

Part of the Robinson conglomerate made its money in textiles. Was it so farfetched that Richard would have traveled to El Salvador twenty-five years ago to make a deal, take a look at a factory, seduce some young, unsuspecting señorita? Probably not.

But then a lot of other Caucasian men might also have reason to visit the same factories, take advantage of the hospitality of the local women.

He pointed this out to Maria.

"He sent money."

Steven couldn't help it. He sat forward in his chair. "Richard Robinson sent money to your mother?"

Her gaze slid away from his. "Someone did."

Steven sat back. "But you have no proof it was him."

77

"No. But it was from an American bank."

"And we're back to crazy," Steven muttered to himself.

"The money stopped last month."

"What else have you got?"

"I have nothing."

"That's the first smart thing you've said. You have nothing. No proof of anything. Even if Richard Robinson fathered you, he's too smart to get caught. Even if he sent your mother money, there won't be a paper trail. Even if he has a scar on his arm that's a dead ringer for this picture you have, it proves nothing. You'd need a paternity test to prove anything, and I can guarantee Lesley will never agree to it. No court in the country will force her to do so based on the flimsy evidence you think you have. So let me give you a piece of advice, Maria. Go back to El Salvador and make a nice life for yourself there. Willow Bay is not the place for you."

"My son is here. *Our* son is here."

"Ah, geez." Steven stood and slammed his glass on the bar. "Our son is a mistake that shouldn't have happened. He isn't *ours* anyway. I never wanted him, and you gave him up. He belongs to Lesley."

"I want to see him."

"Take it up with Lesley."

"I already did."

Steven sneered. "Let me guess. She told you no way in hell would she let you near that kid, am I right?"

"Yes."

"Go home, Maria. There's nothing for you here." Steven opened the door and waited while she gathered her things.

"You are wrong. There is nothing for me there. Everything I want is here." She trailed her fingertips down his chest. "You think only how I can be wrong. But you can think what if I'm right?" He held his breath until she gave him a coquettish smile and sauntered out.

He closed the door and let out a frustrated sigh. He'd gotten her bounced out of the country once, and he'd tied everything up in a neat bow. Now she planned to start tugging on the strings. She could easily unravel everything he'd been rebuilding the past six years.

He'd have to deal with Maria. It was as simple, and as complicated, as that.

Chapter Eight

As Niko approached the podium at the entrance to the plush dining room of the Royal Cove Club, he was certain he didn't imagine the host's raised eyebrow. Lesley told him to wear a jacket, but she hadn't said anything about a tie. He hoped he didn't need one. He'd acquired the navy-blue sports coat last year, at a major department store's end of season sale. He'd paired it with khakis and a white dress shirt open at the collar. When he left the house, he'd thought he looked good enough for lunch at her country club. It never occurred to him that the host would be as well-dressed as the patrons.

It wasn't the first time someone like this guy looked at him with disdain. Not in the moneyed piece of south Florida paradise in which he'd landed. Nor would it be the last. Mostly he'd learned to ignore the attitudes of such individuals and pretend he belonged wherever he was.

"May I help you, sir?"

The guy had to be at least forty. His gold-plated name tag read Marcus Turner. Maybe he managed the dining room or something. Niko didn't know. But the man's tone suggested there was absolutely nothing he'd be able to do for Niko and that most likely he'd mistakenly wandered into the dining room instead of the kitchen.

Niko grinned. He couldn't help picturing Marcus having a stroke when he told him whom he was there to meet. "I'm joining Lesley Robinson for lunch."

"Ahhh." Marcus gave Niko another appraising once-over. "Your name, sir?"

"Morales." Niko purposely rolled the *R* just to mess with him.

The host glanced at his reservation book, running his finger down the entries. "Ah, yes. Here we are. Please follow me, Mr. Morales."

The dining room wasn't crowded. Niko supposed most clubs of this caliber were probably standing room only between January and April, but they didn't do much business during the summer and fall.

Marcus paused at a window table for four in the far corner. He pulled a chair back for Niko and whisked away two of the place settings before promising a server would be right over.

Niko made himself comfortable. The window overlooked a vast swimming pool surrounded by white lounge chairs and umbrella tables for four. A private beach stretched beyond the pool. Both were deserted. After a female server appeared, he ordered iced tea. It was his day off, and he vaguely wished Lesley had suggested meeting at Señor Tequilas, in which case he'd have ordered a beer. But he wasn't calling the shots at the moment. He knew iced tea was the safest beverage choice for a business meeting.

It came served in a frosted glass with a sprig of mint. What the hell was he supposed to do with the mint leaf? Leave it in the glass? Fish it out and set it on his bread plate? No matter how many etiquette books he read, some small detail of proper behavior always escaped him. He decided to leave the leaf in the glass and turned it so he could drink from the other side.

Lesley appeared and Niko watched her greet the snotty host, who seemed absolutely delighted to see her. She wore another of those slim skirts, this one in a narrow black pinstripe paired with a white blouse and peep-toe black pumps. Her hair was upswept and clipped tight. Her only jewelry was a tank watch with a black band and gold hoop earrings.

Niko'd heard the term *understated elegance* before; that's what she made him think of now. Classy. Rich. She didn't flaunt her wealth. Her outfit and her demeanor said it all.

She briefly greeted some of the diners at the other tables, mostly older men and a few couples, before making her way to her own table. Niko knew enough to push his chair out and stand to greet her. He caught the flare of surprise when he did so. But she smiled and touched his arm, briefly pressing her cheek against his. "I'm so glad you could make it."

He didn't have time to contemplate his reaction to the whiff of her subtle perfume. He held the chair adjacent to his out for her.

The server appeared in seconds. Lesley glanced at his beverage choice. "I'll have an iced tea as well. Hold the mint." She smiled at the server and then at him. "I don't know why they put a sprig of mint in the iced tea. I'm never quite sure what to do with it."

Niko smiled back at her and made a note to himself to order his tea plain the next time. If there was a next time.

Lesley folded her hands under her chin and regarded him. He held her gaze. He liked looking at her. He liked trying to figure her out. For example, what was going on in her head right now?

"I like you," she said. "I didn't expect to, but I do."

"Thank you, I think. I like you too. I don't recall having any expectations one way or the other about whether I would, though."

Her tea arrived. "Give us a few minutes, would you, Wendy?" she said to the server. "Thank you." She turned back to Niko. "My reputation as an ice-cold bitch didn't precede me, then?"

Niko frowned. He worked at keeping profanity out of his everyday language. Though the term *bitch* was only mildly profane, he found he didn't care to hear Lesley use it, especially not in reference to herself. "That's an unflattering and probably inaccurate description of you."

She gave a girlish giggle. "Probably?"

"I don't know you well enough to say whether it's accurate or not."

"But based on your limited knowledge of me, your impression is it's inaccurate. I appreciate that. More than you know."

Usually Niko found small talk difficult and pointless, but with Lesley it was a bit like sparring. She wasn't exactly his opponent, but he looked for ways to pierce her armor just the same. Perhaps she was doing the same with him.

She reached for her menu, so he did too. After they ordered, Lesley said, "I suppose you're wondering why I asked you here today?"

"Was it so Mr. Gracious there at the host stand could decide if my sports coat would offend any of the other patrons?"

Her eyes widened. "Of course not! Was Marcus rude to you?"

"No. Come on, Lesley. Most of the Latinos allowed on the property are washing dishes or pruning the bougainvillea. They aren't the guests of Lesley Robinson."

"Sorry. I didn't think about that. The club is just the easiest place for me to do lunch meetings. Are you uncomfortable here?"

"It's fine. I just enjoy yanking your chain."

Lesley glanced around the dining room. "Frankly, I think the club could do with a bit more diversity."

"I'm on the waiting list."

Lesley laughed out loud. It sounded real and genuine to Niko's ears, and it made him smile. He'd like to hear her laugh more often.

She settled back in her chair. Niko again wondered if she ever completely relaxed. She fiddled with her silverware for a moment before she looked at him. "I have a proposition for you."

He kept his gaze on her, wondering where this was going.

"I've been thinking about your community center quite a lot recently. The Robinson Foundation funds will help, of course, but frankly, I know everyone who's anyone in this town. I believe, if you were introduced to people with money and influence in the proper circumstances, by someone they know, you'll soon have more than enough funding to get the center opened."

"The someone being you."

"Yes."

Niko sensed a trap of some sort. "And the 'proper

circumstances'?"

Lesley licked her lips. The quick dart of the tip of her tongue mesmerized Niko. Was she trying to seduce him? He almost laughed out loud at the very idea.

"I don't know how much you know about how things are done here in Willow Bay. There's a rather small, tightly knit group of individuals who basically scratch each other's backs. They all sit on each other's boards, attend each other's golf tournaments and charitable balls. Write checks to each other's causes. Most of the big events occur during the height of the season. Things like the Heart Ball, the Emerald Ball—"

"The Annual Garden Party, the Sunshine Festival."

"Exactly."

Niko didn't bother to tell Lesley he'd worked both traffic and crowd control at those same events.

Their meals arrived. Niko looked at his steak sandwich. It looked decidedly unmanageable with grilled onions, peppers and melted cheese spilling out from beneath the bun. He wondered if he was supposed to pick it up and eat it or leave it on the plate and use a knife and fork. Why was nothing simple here in the land of the rich and influential?

He didn't have money to blow on dry-cleaning his sports coat. He picked up his utensils and leaned toward Lesley. "You're setting me up for something. Why don't you cut to the chase?"

He sliced into the tender steak of the sandwich before realizing he didn't need the knife.

"You're very sharp, Mr. Morales. I need to remember that." Lesley speared a bit of salad on the end of her fork.

Niko finished his first bite. "Isn't that how business

works? I wanted something from you. Now you want something from me. I'm not as sharp as you think, though, because I haven't figured out what it is you want."

"I'd like you to be my escort."

Niko almost choked on his second bite. He managed to swallow it and drink some tea. "I'm sorry. Did you say escort? As in *service*? Sorry, Miss Robinson. I'm not for sale. If you'll excuse me."

He laid his napkin next to his plate and pushed his chair back. Lesley seized his wrist. "I didn't say escort service. I said escort. As in dinner companion. Dance partner." She glanced around the dining room. "Sit down," she hissed. "People are staring."

Niko resumed his seat and placed his napkin across his lap. He made no move to continue eating. Instead he simply stared at Lesley.

She leaned against the back of her chair and lifted her chin. "I am obligated to attend all of those events. It's expected. It comes with the territory of being a member of my family. We are part of this community. My mother is involved in planning numerous events each year. I'm expected to be involved also, or to at least be a presence." She glanced out the window. Niko thought he saw something sad and lonely flit across her features before she looked back at him. "I usually attend these events alone. I don't have the opportunity to meet many men, many appropriate men, er, men I would consider…"

"Worthy of you?"

Lesley lifted her chin even higher. "It's a good thing you smiled when you said that. Otherwise I'd make you sorry."

Niko chuckled and picked up his fork. He wondered what she thought she could do to make him sorry for speaking out of turn. Immediately following that thought came the answer. She'd make sure the board withdrew its support. There went his funding.

A light bulb came on as what she was offering sank in. She'd introduce him to all her rich, influential friends who would donate money to the center, *if* he attended all those balls and parties with her. At least that's what he thought she was getting at.

"May I continue?"

Niko gestured with his fork for her to do so.

"As I was saying, I don't meet many suitable men in my age bracket who would, who could—"

"Make themselves presentable?" Niko grinned. He couldn't help it. He tried to remember when he'd had such a good time.

He'd flustered Miss Iceberg.

"Are you blushing?"

She did that thing again where she squeezed his wrist, except this time she kept her hand there. "Niko, please. This isn't easy for me."

"Sorry. I'll stop interrupting."

"What I was trying to say is yes, it's a bit of a quid pro quo situation, but I honestly thought if you'd do me the favor of escorting me to these events during the upcoming season, I would be happy to introduce you around, get the word out about the Challenge Project, help you with the donation process."

Niko addressed what was left of his sandwich and fries while he thought about Lesley's proposal. Wendy brought a fresh glass of iced tea and whisked away the half full one. He'd say one thing about the Royal Cove

Club. The service was as excellent as the food.

"Well?"

He set his fork down. "Tell me the rest of it."

He gave her credit. Lesley didn't act like she didn't know what he was talking about. "You'd need formal wear."

"Forget it then. I can't afford it."

"I'd be happy to—"

"No."

"Why not?" she quietly exploded. "If it means you can save the kids you say you want to help, then—"

Niko leveled a look at her, and she stopped speaking. It was nice to know he still had the look. He'd used it a lot in his youth. He found it preferable to using his fists or a knife. He'd silenced a lot of punks with the look.

Lesley turned her gaze away from him to the view outside. Her chin dropped a couple of degrees. Her spine softened. She blinked several times.

"You're not going to cry, are you?" he asked.

She glared at him, even while fighting tears.

"Please don't."

She gazed out the window again until she got her control back. Spine straight. Chin up.

"You're right. It was a stupid, selfish idea. I didn't think about how offensive it would sound. I thought only of myself and how I abhor attending all of those things alone. There's a very narrow dating pool in this town for women like me. Mostly it consists of my peers' ex-husbands or possibly a tennis or golf pro from one of the clubs. But even then..." She'd barely touched her salad, but she pushed it away.

"You weren't only thinking of yourself," Niko

corrected her. "You were thinking of me, and you were thinking about all the guys the center can help if I get enough funding to build it.

"But I'm really not comfortable with this. You're not exactly bribing a law enforcement officer, but any perception of impropriety on my part? Not only will it get me fired, but I can kiss the Challenge Project goodbye."

"Those are risks, you're right." Lesley fidgeted with her remaining silverware. "No one has to know about our arrangement. I trust you. I hope you feel you can trust me. But I'll understand if you'd rather not do this."

Lesley presented him with an easy out, but Niko didn't want to let it go. "Maybe I can afford a rental."

Lesley's look of dismay said it all. "A rented tux is simply not an acceptable option. Your own formal wear." She waved a hand through the air. "It's non-negotiable. Almost every event is black-tie. You'd also have to drive my car."

"The Lexus?" Niko grinned. "What a hardship."

"You'll do it?"

"Let me think about it."

When Lesley smiled at him, with her real smile, he didn't know why he didn't just tell her yes. He'd already decided he would.

Chapter Nine

"Definitely the Armani."

Niko stared at his mirrored image and silently agreed with Lesley's decision. He'd always thought one tuxedo looked exactly like every other because he'd always viewed them on a television screen, or more recently when he'd worked an event like the ones he'd soon be attending in Willow Bay.

But he knew now there were subtle differences in the cut, the quality, the fit. The small details made a world of difference. His gaze met Lesley's in the mirror, and she smiled. "Don't you think?"

"Me owning a tux. Has hell frozen over?"

"This one," she said to the hovering salesman. "Send in the tailor."

"Yes, ma'am."

After the salesman left, Lesley approached and stood in front of him. She adjusted the lapels, although in Niko's opinion they needed no adjustment. The jacket fit like it had been made for him. The tailor needed only to hem the pants. Lesley brushed imaginary lint off the front of the suit and stepped back. "It's perfect on you."

"Thank you."

They'd driven to Miami, to a store she knew of near South Beach. She'd made an appointment, and Niko watched her take charge with the salesman, approving and rejecting various options before they adjourned to the changing room. He'd modeled three suits for her, the Armani being the last. She'd chosen shoes and a shirt as well. He'd been dismayed to discover he'd have to learn how to tie a bow tie. He thought they came pre-tied and adjustable.

"Can't I just wear a clip-on?"

Lesley gave him the same look as when he'd suggested renting a tux.

"Fine." Somehow he managed to keep the annoyance out of his tone.

He allowed the salesman to give him a quick lesson. After the tailor stepped in, Lesley never took her gaze off Niko. The older man tugged and smoothed and adjusted the jacket. He turned Niko to the side and did something with the material above the slit at the bottom of the jacket to make it even more flattering. "A slight adjustment, here, I think." He glanced at Niko for approval, who then looked at Lesley. She nodded.

"Yes," Niko agreed.

The tailor pinned and then hung the jacket on a wooden hanger before turning back to assess the fit of the pants. Again he tugged at material just below the knee, then tugged at the waistband in back. Another subtle adjustment of the material there, and miraculously Niko saw the improvement in the fit.

"Yes," he said before the tailor asked. His gaze flickered to Lesley's, and she smiled another of those genuine smiles. He grinned. He hadn't expected to enjoy this outing quite so much.

Next came the hem, which took the tailor only a few moments to pin.

****

While Niko changed, Lesley browsed the display cases of accessories and tried to calm her heated thoughts. Every time she was in Niko's company, she found herself more and more attracted to him, even though they were worlds apart in so many ways.

Niko in formal wear? Her heart almost stopped when she'd pretended to adjust his lapels and brush lint off his jacket. She'd wanted to get closer to him and used an age-old ploy to do so and wondered if he'd seen right through her. She forced herself to step back when she did and pretend a nonchalance she didn't feel.

The elegant clothes did something special for Niko. The clothes gave him the persona of a gentleman, but they couldn't hide the rough edges underneath. They did nothing to hide what kind of shape he was in, either. With his dark hair and eyes and olive skin, Lesley realized she might be competing for his attention at the upcoming events. She certainly wouldn't be the only unattached female in attendance.

"See anything else you have to have?" Niko's voice purred next to her, and she caught herself before she let him know he'd startled her. She looked at him, and the words appeared like a thought bubble over her head but luckily didn't make it to her tongue. *Just you.*

"You'll need cuff links. And studs."

His mouth gaped like a landed trout. "Excuse me?"

Lesley smiled. "Studs. For the shirt. They're like buttons. Want to pick some out?"

Niko's gaze flickered over the display case she indicated. "Let's eat and do it when we come back, okay?"

"Sure."

Lesley arranged for same-day tailoring so they

could take the suit with them.

****

Niko sighed in frustration. He stared at his mirrored reflection in the bathroom in disgust. He'd overcome so much. Fought his way out of poverty and ignorance. He'd worked and read and done everything he could think of to improve himself, his own lot in life and that of others like him. Yet the smallest things, like tying a stupid bow tie, set him back, reminding him he hadn't come as far as he liked to think.

He stood in the bathroom and untied the clumsy bow he'd made for perhaps the tenth time. Propped on the small vanity was a library book open to a page offering a diagram with step-by-step instructions on how to properly tie the perfect bow. He'd come close a couple of times, but his subsequent attempts to get it just right unraveled. The YouTube video he'd watched earlier hadn't helped either. He wanted to give up. He'd have to tell Lesley to forget this whole idea. Somehow he'd have to come up with the money to pay her for the suit. He couldn't imagine the number of off-duty traffic control and security jobs he'd need to do before he accomplished that.

He heard her knock on his front door, just as he tied the tie into another clumsy knot. "I still don't see what's wrong with a clip-on," he grumbled. He doubted anyone would even notice. Or care. Except Lesley.

He padded down the hall in his stockinged feet and opened the door. The emerald-green, floor-length gown with a plunging neckline stopped him in his tracks. She looked smooth and sleek, blond and beautiful. She wore her hair down, coaxed into soft waves that made him think of one of those glam actresses from the forties and fifties. Betty Grable, maybe, or Rita Hayworth. A teardrop-shaped stone suspended from a delicate chain glittered above the vee of her cleavage. Probably a diamond worth about six times what he made in a year.

"Hello there," she said, barely hiding the chuckle beneath her greeting as her gaze zeroed in on his tie.

"Hi," he said glumly as he stepped back to let her in.

He closed the door and they faced each other. "Problems?" she queried, but he saw an amused smile glimmering at the corners of her mouth. What a fool he'd been to think he could move in her circle, that her plan to help him fundraise would ever work. He'd be humiliated. A laughingstock. In fact he already was.

He yanked the tie. "This isn't going to work." He held the tie out to her and she took it. "Let's forget it."

He started back to the bedroom, ready to strip himself out of the suit. At the moment he wanted to throw the entire thing back at her. Jacket, pants, shirt. The ridiculous onyx studs and matching cuff links. He didn't feel elegant at all. He felt clumsy and out of his depth and he didn't like it one bit.

"Such impatience. Remember, we have a deal," Lesley reminded him. He heard the tap of her high heels as she followed him.

He whirled on her. "It's black-tie only, isn't it, this event?" He yanked the tie away from her and waved it in front of her. "It's going to be a problem if I can't figure out how to put the damn thing on."

She bit her lip. He was a hundred percent sure she was trying not to laugh.

"It doesn't help to have you laughing at me." Even he could hear the sulky tone in his voice.

"I'm not laughing at you," she assured him, though her eyes were dancing. "I'm laughing with you."

Niko frowned. There was no malice in her smile. Perhaps she found the situation amusing, but not at his expense. Plus, every time she smiled for real, something inside him responded to it.

"Give me this," she said, reaching for the tie. He let it go.

She reached up, and he bowed his head so she could slip it around his neck. "This isn't going to work," she said.

"Told you so."

Ignoring him, she glanced around. "You'll have to sit down."

He took a seat on a stool at the kitchen counter while Lesley concentrated on his tie. She leaned forward, which offered him an even better view of her cleavage. He sat absolutely still while she worked, mesmerized by the sway of the teardrop necklace and thoughts of what lay beneath the drape of the fabric. He dug his fingers into his thighs to fight the itch to cup her breasts in his hands, to see if they were as soft and real as they appeared to be.

The subtle scent of her perfume invaded his senses, fogging his brain and sending all kinds of lustful signals to the rest of his body. He used a trick he'd used often before. Mentally reciting bits of poetry he'd read, the times tables, the steps of cleaning his service revolver—anything unsexy he could think of so he wouldn't throw caution to the wind and act on his natural impulses.

"There." Lesley straightened and stepped back. Niko let go of a breath he hadn't realized he'd been holding. He reached up to feel what she'd done.

"Really?" He couldn't believe she'd accomplished in two minutes what he'd been struggling with for half an hour. "We're good?"

"We're good," she echoed without a trace of amusement.

"You'll have to teach me how to do that."

"I will."

They regarded each other for long seconds. Several compliments ran through Niko's head, but he didn't think he could pull any of them off without sounding phony. "Nice dress, by the way."

His compliment got another smile out of her. "Thank you."

"I'll get my shoes."

He did so, pausing for a moment to check his appearance in the full-length mirror inside the closet door. The tie was perfect. Maybe he wouldn't fit in with Lesley's crowd, but at least his tux would get a passing grade.

Lesley's gleaming white Lexus sat at the end of the driveway behind his Acura. She handed him the keys, and he opened her door, waiting until she was settled before closing it.

His neighbors, a retired couple named Julio and Martha Perez, waved to him from their front stoop. They often settled there in the early evenings, so Niko knew they were taking in every detail and would likely share each one with the other neighbors. It couldn't be helped, and it wouldn't matter anyway. He liked his neighbors, but he didn't feel compelled to explain himself to them.

He shrugged out of his jacket and laid it in the

backseat. Somewhere he'd seen it suggested to do so to keep the jacket from wrinkling.

Lesley waited patiently for him to get behind the wheel and adjust the seat. Once they were on their way, he said, "How many of these things did you say we'll be attending?"

"Several. Tonight's just the beginning, actually. The Emerald Ball's one of the smaller ones, but it's a good place to start. A warm-up if you will. Next will be the Sneaker Ball."

"The Sneaker Ball?"

"It benefits disabled children in the area. It's formal, but guests decorate and wear sneakers. Usually a few celebrities are recruited, and their sneakers are auctioned off as part of the fund-raising.

"Later in the season are the bigger, heavy-hitting events. The Angel Ball, which raises scholarships for a couple of the local college prep schools, and the Heart Ball, which funds the hospital's heart institute. I'll give you a schedule."

"So I should have put together a ball to raise money for the community center instead of attending all these other balls to meet people to donate money to it?"

Lesley glanced at him. "Even if you did, you'd have a difficult time raising money. No one who's anyone with any money or clout would attend."

"How do you know?"

"Niko, trust me. I know how things work in this town. First you have to get your project off the ground, which takes money. Lots and lots of donated money. The people who donate to what they consider a worthy cause are those you'll meet at these events this season. They'll give for a couple of reasons. One will be because of me, because of who my family is and what it stands for. Another will be because of you: who you are and where you came from, and what you're trying to do. The third reason is because your cause is worthwhile. Really, truly worthwhile. But the movers and shakers don't move quickly. They're cautious, especially when it comes to money. They don't want to be scammed or made fools of. They'll support you, but not until they trust you."

****

Niko had been tempted to interrupt Lesley more than once during her speech, but he was glad he'd held back. He knew she spoke the truth. It all came down to trust. He couldn't lose sight of that. He wouldn't get caught up in the posturing he'd seen glimpses of in the past, where people pretended to be what they weren't, believing they could gain some kind of advantage.

He pulled her car under the porte cochere at the entrance to the Willow Bay Beach Club Hotel. A valet dressed in white darted around the front of the car to take the keys while another opened Lesley's door. Niko retrieved his jacket and pocketed the claim ticket.

He offered Lesley his arm, and they entered the hotel. At the top of the grand staircase were registration tables where they stopped for drink tickets and table assignments. Bars were set up in the reception area and servers were circulating with trays of canapés.

"Would you like a drink?" he asked as he steered Lesley away from the tables with a hand on the middle of her back.

"I find a glass or two of wine makes these events much more bearable. I'd love a pinot grigio."

"Pinot grigio it is." They made their way to the line

in front of one of the bars. A couple of female acquaintances greeted Lesley, and they exchanged air kisses.

"Meet Niko Morales," Lesley said. "Niko, this is Sissy Spano and Myra Daniels."

Niko inclined his head. "Ladies."

Their gazes moved from Lesley to Niko and back. Sissy leaned toward Lesley and said none too subtly, "We'll talk. Nice to meet you. Niko, was it?" They moved back into the crush. Lesley arranged their arrival approximately halfway into the cocktail hour. Apparently most of the other guests had the same idea, for the crowd had grown substantially in the past few minutes.

The bartender placed napkins in front of them. "Wine for the lady," Niko said. "I don't suppose you have light beer?"

"Of course, sir."

Niko handed Lesley her glass and gave two drink tickets to the bartender. He dropped a five-dollar bill into the oversize glass goblet at the end of the bar. "Thank you, sir," said the bartender.

Niko nodded and picked up his bottle of beer. He didn't intend to drink much, but he'd found tipping wait staff beneficial, especially when he needed information.

He kept close to Lesley as she moved through the crowd. She stopped or was stopped often by other guests. She introduced him each time, offering tidbits of information about her acquaintances. He shook hands with the men and politely greeted the women. He couldn't miss the speculative glances sent toward them.

After half an hour, chimes sounded and the ballroom doors were thrown open. The servers politely indicated to the guests that the cocktail reception was over and they were to find their tables.

Not surprisingly, their table for ten was at the front, close to the stage and the dance floor. Lesley set her nearly empty glass down at one of the settings and placed her evening bag on the chair. Niko set the beer he'd been nursing at the setting next to hers.

Another couple chose seats across from them, so Niko followed Leslie while introductions were made. Soon the other seats filled. More introductions were made until finally, mercifully, everyone was seated.

An older gentlemen stepped up to the podium on the stage and made some opening remarks, welcoming everyone to the event. An invocation followed. A small band with a female vocalist began to play soft rock classics. Servers streamed out with the salad course. Diners were offered a choice of red or white wine, and requests were taken for a fish or meat entrée.

Niko declined the wine, chose the fish, and watched Lesley in action. She was charming and graceful. She put everyone at the table at ease, asking those closest to her leading questions and keeping the conversation flowing by appearing genuinely interested in their answers.

The woman next to him engaged her husband and the couple on the other side in conversation, so Niko relaxed. He didn't have to contribute anything, just smile politely. He didn't think he'd ever smiled so much in one hour as he had tonight.

Once everyone had been served and the wine poured, the salads were addressed. Niko was glad he'd reviewed place settings earlier and he knew which fork to use. He quietly ate the unimpressive salad and listened in on two different conversations.

When he'd finished, he set the fork on his plate and pushed it slightly away. Lesley leaned close. "Everything all right?"

"Great. Wonderful. Fantastic."

She frowned slightly. "What's the matter?" she whispered.

He leaned toward her and did something he'd been wanting to do. He tucked a wavy strand of hair behind her ear, letting the silk of it slide through his fingers. He put his mouth to her ear and whispered, "I'm bored."

She burst out laughing, and he sat back, grinning at her reaction. Her laughter caught the attention of everyone else at the table.

"You have to let the rest of us in on the joke now," insisted Doug Snyderman, who was seated across from her.

The others chimed in in agreement.

"Should I tell them?" Lesley asked, sliding a glance in Niko's direction.

"Up to you."

"Niko told me he's bored."

The woman next to him, whose name was Charlene, chuckled. "Oh, darling, you're not the only one."

"Hear, hear," Doug added, as the others murmured their agreement.

"In fact, Niko's been thinking about planning his own event," Lesley continued. "Much more fun, he assures me."

Niko sent an amused look her way.

"Really, Niko?" Charlene said. "Tell us. We've been doing the same old thing for years, it seems.

Everyone pretends they've planned something new and different, added an unusual twist to their event, but I swear it's all been done before."

"We need some fresh blood. Some new ideas." This came from Doug's wife, Marsha. "Tell us what you've got in mind."

He glanced at Lesley again. Was she serious? Were they? She nodded like she knew what he was going to say. Like they'd discussed it already, which they hadn't. In fact, Niko would have to make it up as he went along, but he decided to follow through on a glimmer of an idea he'd had after Lesley's speech in the car.

"A salsa competition."

"Salsa?" Doug boomed. "With tortilla chips?"

Niko chuckled. "No, but that's not a bad idea. Salsa. Dancing."

"A dance competition?" said Charlene's husband, Mitchell. "That'll be a tough sell. To the men anyway."

"Not if we have a few young and cute female instructors to teach them the steps."

Mitchell leaned forward. "Okay. I'm listening." Everyone chuckled at his earnestness.

"Of course, we'd also have to find some young, good-looking male instructors for the ladies," Niko said

"Now you're talking," Charlene and Marsha put in simultaneously. More laughter followed.

"Instead of *Dancing with the Stars*, maybe we can do it outdoors. Dancing Under the Stars." Niko began to seriously warm to the idea, which took shape the more he spoke. "I say we ditch the black ties."

"Hear, hear," Doug and Mitch said.

"Everyone wears something loose and comfortable.

Clothes they can dance in. In fact, we could add on a dance costume competition. Give out trophies for all kinds of stuff. Best dressed couple. Most unusual outfit. Back to your idea, Doug, we serve chips and salsa. Margaritas. Tequila. Mexican beers. Sangria."

"We'll call it the Salsa Ball," Lesley put in. "No, wait. The Salsa Bowl!" She patted Niko's wrist in her excitement, which made everyone laugh.

The servers cleared the salad plates and began serving the entrees.

"Throw in an auction. A trip to Spain. Or a stay at one of those resorts in Cancun or Porta Vallarta," Charlene suggested. "Maybe a cruise with stops in Mexico."

"Cooking lessons, dance lessons, Spanish lessons, for that matter," Kate Keller added. "I'd love to know what my cleaning lady is saying."

"I'd like to be able to communicate with the landscapers," her husband Bob said.

"I love the whole idea," Candace Mueller broke in. "It does sound different and fun. But what would you be raising money for, Niko?"

Just like that, Lesley had set him up—and it was perfect. She'd given him the ideal opening. Everyone at the table was already on his side. They were interested in what he had to say. Now it was up to him to keep the ball rolling.

Over the entrees, he outlined the Challenge Project and why it was so important. The men at the table asked most of the questions, but the women had a few as well. By the time the plates were cleared, Doug had suggested Niko put together a presentation for his men's club, and Mitch wanted information on becoming a corporate sponsor. "Great PR for a firm like ours," he said.

When dessert and coffee arrived, table-hopping began, along with restroom and smoke breaks or another trip to the bars.

"Don't we have to go socialize?" Niko asked Lesley after he'd noticed the mass exodus from their table. "Make some more contacts?"

"They'll come to us," Lesley informed him.

"How can you be so sure?"

"Because Sissy Spano and Myra Daniels will have told everyone I'm here with you."

"Of course. Now they're all dying to meet me."

"Exactly." She looked over his left shoulder and without moving her lips said, "Uh-oh. Brace yourself."

Before Niko could blink, a woman swathed in a shimmering gold gown wrapped her arms around Lesley and pressed her cheek against hers. "Darling! Are you having a wonderful time? You didn't tell me you'd found an escort." She winked at Niko as she straightened. "You must introduce me."

He stood, then helped Lesley with her chair. "Mother, meet Niko Morales. Niko, my mother, Mitzi."

"Pleased to meet you, Mrs. Robinson."

"Oh, please. Mrs. Robinson makes me sound ancient, which I assure you I am not. Or a seducer of young men, which I assure you I am. It's Mitzi. Especially for you."

He was beginning to understand Lesley's various smiles. The cool, reserved one she used for business settings. The polite, slightly warmer one she brought out for social occasions such as this. The genuine one that gave him glimpses of what he thought of as the real

Lesley who lived somewhere beneath her carefully constructed facade.

Mitzi Robinson wasn't drunk, but she was tipsy. Niko caught the speculative, calculating gleam in her eye as she assessed him. "Wherever did my daughter find you? Niko, is it?"

"Actually, I found her. And may I say I'm quite happy I did."

Mitzi's gaze shifted to Lesley, who offered her nothing but a cool smile. Before she could say more, another couple edged closer, angling for an introduction. After that came an endless parade of people who wanted to meet Lesley Robinson's mystery date. Niko knew he'd never remember most of them or be able to put a name with each face, but he also knew Lesley had his back. That was enough to let him relax into a situation he'd otherwise have found uncomfortable in the extreme.

When finally it seemed he'd met everyone in the room and the crowd began to thin, it was time to leave. While he waited for Lesley to visit the ladies' room, it occurred to him that he'd actually enjoyed himself. He'd been thinking these social gatherings would be unpleasant necessities he'd have to weather in order to achieve his goals. If he were on his own, that would probably have been true. But having Lesley at his side, championing his cause, watching his back, made all the difference. He owed her. Usually he didn't like owing anyone. But with her it didn't bother him at all.

She appeared in front of him almost as if he'd conjured her with his thoughts. "You're deep in thought."

"I was thinking about you."

Her eyes lit as bright as her smile. "Really?"

"Thank you."

He bent and kissed her cheek. He didn't think about it; he just did it. Even that tiny, impersonal touch got to him. He already knew how silky her hair was. So was her skin. The scent of her perfume had faded, but the barest whiff almost sent him reeling.

She appeared puzzled. "For what?"

"Everything," he said simply. "Ready to go?"

There was a queue in the valet line. Every valet hustled to retrieve cars and collect tips. The departing guests were subdued, chatting quietly in small groups or waiting silently with a spouse.

"Good evening, Lesley. You're looking well."

A man whom Niko had not met inside pressed a lingering kiss near her temple. Her hand was nestled in the crook of Niko's arm, and she tightened her fingers around his elbow. Even if she hadn't, he'd have sensed her tension.

"Steven," she said coolly, then made a pointed attempt to ignore him.

The man was having none of it. He stared at Niko. "Where are your manners, Lesley? Aren't you going to introduce me to your, ah, date?"

She sent him a look close to a glare. "Niko Morales, Steven Lambert."

Even Niko was aware of the interested looks directed their way from the others waiting for their vehicles to appear. He did not offer his hand but merely inclined his head in Lambert's direction.

"Morales, eh? Seems to me we've met somewhere before."

"I doubt it," Niko and Lesley said at the same time,

then grinned at each other.

The line moved forward, but Steven stayed with them. "What line of work are you in, Morales? Landscaping? Produce? Ditch digging?"

"Steven!" Lesley hissed.

Niko didn't know what the guy's problem was, but he knew better than to be goaded into a physical confrontation. "I'm a cop."

"Ah. For a moment there I was afraid you'd stooped to sleeping with the hired help." This he directed at Lesley.

"I believe that's your specialty," she said.

As if by divine intervention, her Lexus appeared on the drive in front of them. The valet handed the keys to Niko and opened Lesley's door. Neither of them said goodbye to Steven.

"What a prick," Niko commented as he accelerated down the hotel's sloping driveway.

"You have no idea."

"You know him well?"

Lesley turned to look out of the window. "He's my ex-husband."

"*That* guy? I think I pulled him over for some minor traffic violation a while ago."

She faced forward. "I hope you don't think less of me."

"Why? Because you married a jerk and then had sense enough to get rid of him? Of course not. My past relationships aren't exactly something I'm proud of."

"Thank you."

"For what?"

"Not judging me."

"It's not my place."

"Too bad the rest of Willow Bay doesn't think like you do."

"You're the one who has to live with your choices. As long as you're okay with them, it doesn't matter what anyone else thinks. Or says."

Lesley leaned her head back against the seat and smiled at him. "How'd you get so smart?"

Niko flashed her a grin. "I read a lot."

Chapter Ten

Niko's phone rang just as he started the dryer. A day off meant laundry, cleaning house, and a trip to the supermarket. He didn't recognize the number but answered anyway. "Morales."

"Niko?"

"Yes."

"It's Kate Keller calling. We met at the Emerald Ball."

Kate Keller stood out in his memory because of her close-cropped white hair and Pilates-honed figure. "Yes, of course. How are you?"

"I'm well. The reason I'm calling is Marsha Snyderman and I talked after the ball and we've decided we'd like to organize the Salsa Bowl."

"That's great. You have a year to plan it?"

"We'd like to do it this year, actually. With your approval, of course."

Niko sank onto one of the stools in the kitchen. "I'm...sure, but I thought all the big places were booked. I thought you had to plan events like this way ahead of time."

"Usually, that's true. Most of the regular venues are booked this season, but we thought we'd try something different because the Salsa Bowl's going to be an entirely different kind of gathering."

"What did you have in mind?"

"Niko, we've got a *ton* of ideas we're dying to discuss with you. Would you be free by any chance to join us for dinner this evening at the Royal Cove Club? Bob and Doug will be there too, of course. You won't believe this, but they're dying to get involved as well."

"Wow, Kate. That sounds great."

"We'll see you then? Around seven in the lounge? Oh, jacket and tie required."

"Of course. I'll see you then."

Niko hung up and looked around at his humble abode. He could hardly believe what had happened since he'd met Lesley. The challenges he'd expected to get the community center up and running were falling by the wayside. The hardest, finding funding, just became easier. Now he'd have the kind of support from the kind of people in Willow Bay he needed. He owed Lesley.

Big time.

****

Lesley entered the Royal Cove Club, scanning for her mother. Thursday evenings were traditionally spent having drinks and dinner at the club with friends. Mitzi never missed an opportunity to socialize. She could hardly blame her. A pall had fallen over the Robinson estate since Richard's return from the rehab center with his nursing staff and strict schedules. And a recent complication kept him out of his wheelchair and bedridden.

Lesley was less inclined to go out on a regular basis, but she often gave in to Mitzi's pleas and joined her, especially if it was with Becky and Walter Collins who were old and dear family friends. Walter was chairman of the most successful independent bank headquartered in Willow Bay. Becky sat on the boards of several charitable foundations, most notably Willow Bay Hospital and the local shelter for abused women. Her outgoing personality balanced Walter's more serious tone. They'd been college sweethearts and now had four grown children and eight grandchildren.

Lesley wanted to spend some time with Ricky before she left since she wouldn't be there to tuck him in tonight. She'd been making more of an effort to forge a bond with him, to spend quality time with him every day. This afternoon they walked the beach together. She found him more willing to open up to her in such a setting, telling her bits and pieces about his teachers and what went on at school.

She'd showered and zipped herself into a black cocktail dress and added minimal jewelry, just enough to accent. She wanted a glass of wine and one of the club's exquisitely simple and delicious entrees, and to make an early night of it.

She peeked into the lounge, never sure if her mother and the Collinses might still be enjoying the cocktail hour or if they'd already been seated. She saw the Kellers and the Snydermans holding court at the bar, but someone else was with them, someone she hadn't expected to see.

Niko.

She couldn't help but stare. She had to convince herself her eyes weren't playing tricks on her and put the brakes on the flutter of excitement running through her. He wore the same sports coat as when she'd first met him, paired with a light blue tie and dark gray slacks. His hair gleamed, and his smile flashed at something Doug said. Lesley caught herself staring.

He noticed her, probably because she *was* staring, and waved a hand in greeting. She got hold of herself and joined the group, everyone bussing cheeks and sharing greetings. Niko was last. He pressed his cheek to hers—oh, how quickly he learned the gestures of her circle. She drank in the subtle citrusy scent that clung to him. Lesley could never figure out if it was soap or cologne, but whatever it was made her want to get closer to him.

"We're doing some preliminary planning for the Salsa Bowl," Marsha bubbled. "You should join us. Niko needs a dinner partner."

"Oh." Lesley eyed Niko in confusion. "I would, but I'm meeting my mother and some friends for dinner." She tried in vain to stamp down the surge of jealousy shooting through her. Niko had infiltrated her world, her social circle. Without her.

True, she'd made the introductions, her aim to help him navigate his way through the country club set and build support for his cause. But she'd expected to be by his side along the way. She'd found him, after all. She'd created him in a way, for Pete's sake. She'd paid for the damn tuxedo that let him access the event where he'd met the Kellers and the Snydermans in the first place.

As soon as she had those thoughts, she felt ashamed of herself. She hadn't expected him to be in awe of her while she personally handled everything for him, had she? That was the kind of nonsense she found out too late Steven expected from her.

She'd bought Niko a suit and offered him guidance, but she wasn't responsible for his success or failure with the Challenge Project. He'd have succeeded with or without the Robinson Family Foundation's support. She'd recognized his inner drive. He wouldn't give up on something until he got what he wanted. He'd do it his way.

"Maybe I can make the next meeting. If I have enough advance notice." She addressed this statement to the group, but she made sure her gaze rested longest on Niko.

He gave her one of those knowing grins as if he'd followed her train of thought from start to finish. "We wouldn't think of proceeding without you, would we?"

The others jumped in to agree, and Kate said, "We only called Niko this afternoon, as a matter of fact."

Lesley breathed a sigh of relief. This was an impromptu meeting. She knew how impetuous Kate could be, so she wasn't surprised.

"I'd best find my mother. It was lovely seeing you all." She was sure Niko's gaze followed her all the way to the dining room and smiled at the warmth the thought gave her.

Chapter Eleven

The moment Mitch took up residence in the guest house, Lesley, Lita, and Mitzi seemed to breathe a collective sigh of relief. He began dropping off and picking up Ricky from school. Mitch didn't have children, but Lesley could tell he would have made a great father by the way he treated Ricky. They became pals just as easily as Ricky and Niko had. Mitch was more available, however, since he lived on the premises, so he and Ricky often kicked the soccer ball around or built things with Ricky's Legos.

Mitch coordinated his schedule with Lita's so one of them was always there to receive callers and deliveries. The driveway gate stayed closed otherwise.

He usually arrived in the kitchen after everyone else finished breakfast. Lesley noticed her mother tended to linger and was secretly amused. One could hardly blame Mitzi. Even though she was married and Lesley knew her mother would remain faithful to her father, Mitzi was a woman who attracted and enjoyed male attention. Mitch was not immune to her charms, as Lesley had noticed the day she'd introduced them.

Where was the harm, she mused as she finished her coffee and brought up today's schedule on her iPad. Ricky brushed his teeth while Lita packed his lunch. Mitch took a seat at the table, with his travel mug full of coffee, to wait for the boy, and engaged Mitzi in idle conversation.

Lesley's ears perked up when she heard Mitzi mention the upcoming Angel Ball. "Most men avoid these events like the plague unless they have a very good reason to attend," her mother told Mitch. "Like a wife who insists or a company who has a table to fill. I can't say I blame them. So many of the balls are a dead bore."

"But they raise a lot of money for some very good causes," he said.

"Of course," Mitzi agreed. "I just wish ..." She propped her chin in one hand and gazed wistfully out the window. "Richard and I used to have such a good time, even if we were bored. We'd play games to see who at our table would make a faux pas, who'd get drunk and behave inappropriately. On the way home we'd joke about the food, the band—oh, every little thing our friends said or did." She glanced back at Mitch. "It sounds silly, doesn't it? But it broke up the monotony and made those evenings more fun."

"Everything's more fun when you share it with someone whose company you enjoy."

"Yes."

"I'm ready, Mitch," Ricky said as he entered the kitchen, towing his backpack. Lita took it from him and loaded his lunch box inside. Mitch got up.

"Bye, Lita. Bye, Missy," Ricky said.

"Goodbye, my little man." Mitzi held out her arms to Ricky for a hug.

"Bye, Mom," he said a bit shyly to Lesley.

Lesley stood and hugged him, kissing the top of his head. "Bye, Ricky. Have a good day."

He beamed at her. "I will."

Lesley refilled her own coffee, glanced at her watch, and returned to her seat. Mitzi gazed at her, a small smile playing around her lips. "What?" Lesley asked.

"Ricky calls you Mom now."

Lesley fiddled with the silverware she hadn't used, then gripped the handle of her coffee cup. "We talked about it a few weeks ago."

Mitzi waited for her to continue. Lita pretended to be busy at the sink. There were no secrets in this house anyway.

"I haven't—I'm not—I'm trying to be a better mother to him, that's all."

She took a sip of her coffee and stared at her iPad. She felt ridiculous and exposed. She and Mitzi weren't close, and Lita was an employee, even though she was considered family. Lesley couldn't imagine baring her soul to either one of them, admitting her sense of inadequacy, her struggle to get past the circumstances of Ricky's birth and love him the way he deserved.

"I think it's wonderful, darling," Mitzi said. Lita turned from the sink and flashed Lesley a quick smile.

"Yes. Well." She stood and picked up her coffee and her iPad. "I have a busy day." She fled to her office. At least there she knew what she was doing. She was in her element. She didn't second-guess every decision she made. Why couldn't she be as capable in her personal life?

****

A few days later, Mitch tapped at her open door late in the afternoon. Lesley looked up from her computer screen and, seeing who it was, smiled and beckoned him to enter. "Everything all right?" she asked as he took a seat across from her.

He shifted a bit in his seat. "Yes. Fine."

Lesley waited, sincerely hoping Mitch wasn't about to resign. He'd fit into the family routine seamlessly. Even in the short time he'd been with them, Lesley had come to rely on him more than she'd expected.

"It's about your mother," he began.

"Is there a problem?"

"No. At least I hope not."

Mitch squirmed a bit more. Lesley waited. She was ready to call it a day anyway. The only thing she had planned was a glass of wine before dinner. And her usual run afterward.

"The thing is, your mother asked if I'd accompany her to the Heart Ball coming up in February."

"Oh." Lesley saw how such an invitation might put Mitch in an awkward position. He was Lesley's employee and, by extension, Mitzi's. He probably didn't know how to turn her down without offending her or jeopardizing his position with the family. "I'll speak to her," Lesley said. "She shouldn't have made you feel like you're required to escort her—"

"She didn't."

"She didn't? Oh, but I thought—I guess I'm not sure why you're here."

"She said I didn't have to clear it with you, but—"

"You already told her you'd attend with her?" Lesley didn't bother to hide her surprise. Both at Mitzi's boldness and Mitch's acceptance. But in hindsight perhaps she shouldn't have been.

"Is that a problem?"

"No, no, I don't think so."

"Technically, you hired me. I understand I work for the entire family, but I wanted to make sure you approved."

"I'm not going to object, if that's what you're asking."

"But you're not thrilled about it."

"Mitch, my mother does as she pleases. We lead independent lives for the most part. You're both adults. If she invited you and you're willing to attend an event such as this with her, truly, I have no objection."

"I'm strictly going as an escort," Mitch clarified.

Lesley relaxed back into her chair and smiled. "And a friend, I think."

"Of course. I don't want you to think there's anything else going on." He blushed clear to his hairline.

Lesley found his discomfort endearing. "I didn't. Not for a minute."

Mitch grinned. "I just hope I don't embarrass her."

"Are you kidding? My mother will likely be the envy of every other woman there."

After he left, Lesley spun her chair around to gaze out the window at the fountain and landscaping. She recalled her first meeting with Niko and thought back also to the meeting between Mitch and her mother.

She glanced back at her computer screen. Her father had attached a couple of new pages from his memoir to an email. In them he'd described meeting her mother for the first time and how taken with her he'd been. The email message said, *See? Love finds you if you let it.* She'd never thought of her father as a sentimental man, but since the stroke that side of him became more evident.

She and Mitzi were two women who longed for companionship, especially at these formal events. Lesley, of course, also wanted to help Niko raise money for the community center. She smiled a little, remembering his reaction when she made the offer, how his hackles rose, how insulted he'd been. Evidently her mother used more tact when it came to inviting Mitch to accompany her to the Heart Ball.

She hoped her mother made it clear the ball was black-tie only.

****

That evening Mitzi tapped on the door to Lesley's suite. Lesley was just back from her run and ready to take a shower. "Darling, do you have a moment? I wanted to speak to you."

"Of course, Mother. Come in."

Once they were seated, Mitzi said, "I invited Mitch to accompany me to the Heart Ball."

"I know. He told me this afternoon."

"Oh. I didn't realize."

"He assured me he was only going as your friend and companion."

"Well, of course. Surely you don't think I would, that he and I—" Mitzi blushed. "Oh dear."

"Mother, it's fine. And it's really none of my business."

"Of course it's your business. I would never do anything to embarrass you or your father. You do know that, don't you?"

"Yes. I do."

Mitzi gave her a pleading look. "It's just that I get so…"

"Lonely?"

119

Tears glistened in Mitzi's eyes. "I miss your father so much. The way he used to be. How he could walk into a room and command it. Everyone wanted to be part of his circle."

"I remember."

Mitzi sat up straighter. "I get so frustrated with the way things are now."

"So does he."

"Of course." Mitzi paused for a moment. "I want you to know I would never have approached Mitch about going to the ball with me until I talked to your father about it."

"Oh." Lesley was a little taken aback. "And he's all right with it?"

Mitzi smiled sadly. "Your father's a realist. And he understands me." She held Lesley's gaze. "I hope you understand as well."

"Of course."

After Mitzi left, Lesley contemplated her parents' relationship. Her mother had always adored and supported Richard while he in turn treated her as if she were the most rare and special of gems. Now they were separated by an unfathomable gulf, even though they lived under the same roof. Even before the stroke, Lesley noticed how her father's eyes lit up when he saw Mitzi, no matter how tired he was or how bad a day he'd had.

Lesley had wanted the same kind of relationship for herself once. But as each year passed, it seemed less and less likely she'd ever find it.

****

The Heart Ball had been scheduled for February fourteenth. *Lovely*, Leslie thought as she prepared for the evening. Valentine's Day without a Valentine, nor any prospect of one, was depressing. At least she had an escort. That was something, she supposed, not to have to attend this season's events alone.

Niko's popularity increased as the season progressed. He'd made numerous contacts. Each time they were together, he updated her on the funding status for the center. His enthusiasm never waned. Lesley gathered he spent nearly every free moment working toward getting the center up and running. When he did? What then?

She stared at herself in the mirror. She might never see him again. She selected a tube of mascara and started on her lashes, pushing the unwelcome thought away. But it refused to go. She hadn't admitted to anyone how much she looked forward to the evenings she spent with Niko under the guise of simple companionship.

They'd developed a working friendship. Niko was physically attractive, but his pull went beyond that. He had no formal degree, but from what Lesley could tell, he was self-taught and widely read. His kind of street sense could only be learned from experience. He'd smoothed his rough edges but they were there, beneath the surface, and perhaps that was what Lesley found wildly exciting about him. She was tired of refinement. Tired of proper behavior.

"I'm tired of being me," she whispered, staring at herself in the mirror.

She'd become someone she hardly recognized anymore. She'd been presenting the Lesley Robinson facade to the world for so long, she couldn't find the real Lesley buried beneath it. Because that Lesley could be hurt, could be betrayed. That Lesley couldn't trust, couldn't relax, couldn't let go. Or wouldn't let go. That Lesley was afraid.

She tossed the mascara back in its place and picked up a lipstick. Red was not her color, even though it was the Heart Ball's theme. She'd chosen a gown in burgundy and given Niko a tie for his tux to match. She knew heads turned when they were together. Even though they were opposites, they complemented each other.

Back in her bedroom, she removed the dress from its hanger and eyed it critically. It was conservatively sexy, a look she'd pretty much perfected. She'd long subscribed to the theory that less was more when it came to showing skin. The dress fit her like a glove. She had no reason to flaunt what kind of shape she was in.

She dressed quickly and donned the jewelry she'd chosen. She stared at her reflection one final time, turning to check the view from the back. All the while she anticipated Niko's reaction.

If he was attracted to her, he hadn't acted on it. She was sure she'd seen a flare of appreciation in his eyes every time she showed up at his door dressed for an evening out. He complimented her, but it was almost always about her clothing. "Nice dress." "You look nice." "That's a good color on you." Niko behaved as a proper gentleman should. Perhaps he was as good at acting as she was.

Maybe it was time to find out.

****

"Want to dance?" Niko asked three hours later.

A tingle slid through Lesley when Niko had leaned

over to make his request, his lips close to her ear, his warm breath against her neck. "I'd love to."

She and Niko had danced at a couple of other events, keeping a discreet distance from each other. A lady and a gentlemen. The very last thing Lesley wanted was to make a fool of herself and give the gossips something else to talk about. She wasn't immune to the whispers of speculation about her relationship with Niko at every event. The fact that the two of them kept turning up together only fed the rumor mill. Which was another reason Lesley refused to get too close to Niko. One or two dances at each ball meant nothing. Dancing the night away, holding each other too closely, would send tongues wagging and innuendo spreading like wildfire. But Lesley was tired of holding Niko at arm's length. In fact, she wanted to feel the press of his body against hers. She longed for it.

She knew Niko had moves from the few times they'd danced together. Possibly his Latino heritage. He liked music. Lesley's dance training had been more formal. She found it hard to relax the way he did. Her moves were less fluid. She knew she was tense and stiff compared to him, but she couldn't seem to help it.

She drained the rest of her wine, hoping she'd drunk enough to relax on the dance floor. The band began a ballad, and more couples streamed forward.

Niko took her hand and circled his arm around her back as they moved to the center of the floor. He kept a proper distance between them. Lesley stared at his neck above his starched white shirt and burgundy tie. At his earlobe and his sideburn. She drank in the scent of him, felt the heat of his body through his clothes. She closed her eyes and wished he'd ignore propriety and hold her even closer.

Another couple bumped her from behind, pushing her off balance and into Niko. His hold on her tightened, and she got her wish as the other couple whispered their apologies. She was plastered against Niko, and his hand dipped slightly lower on her waist. He looked at her, and she couldn't mistake what she saw in his eyes. Desire. But as quickly as she'd seen it, he smiled and closed the shutters over his interest.

So, it *was* an act. Lesley smiled back. When the ballad ended, a pop song with a driving beat came next, and Niko moved them smoothly into it. She told herself to relax and go with him. For once her self-talk worked. She let go, finding it much easier to follow his lead when she didn't think about it so much. He kept hold of her hand, pushing her to arm's length, spinning her around and bringing her back close to him, never missing a beat. She couldn't stop smiling and the thought struck her: *I'm having fun!* How long had it been since she had? Much, much too long.

"Ready to go?" Niko growled in her ear.

She wouldn't have minded another dance, but something about the way Niko asked the question, something about his mouth so close to her ear, made her say yes without hesitation.

****

The air outside cooled their overheated bodies. Niko removed his jacket while they waited for the valet. He took the wheel of the Lexus, and they were mostly silent on the drive back to his place.

"May I come in for a minute?" Lesley asked when he parked behind his car.

"Sure."

124

The moment Niko closed the door behind them, Lesley's mouth was on his. Her arms came around his neck, and her lithe body pressed against him. Rational thought fled. Instinct took over.

His hands tangled in her hair while their tongues grappled for dominance. Lesley's hair clip fell to the floor with a clatter Niko barely heard. She yanked his shirt out of his waistband. He tried to say something, he didn't know what, but she didn't let him, keeping him distracted with her mouth and her hands. She tugged at the knot on his tie, finally getting it undone.

Cool, refined, reserved Lesley Robinson was seducing him. Niko could hardly wrap his head around it. Truth be told, she'd been seducing him since the moment they'd met, although she probably didn't know that. She'd played a big part in his fantasies of late, mostly because he figured fantasizing was the only way he'd ever have her. But this? This was real. In the tiny part of his brain still functioning, he thought there was something not right about it. They should slow down or stop before this went too far.

Or maybe not, he decided when her hand cupped him, sending his erection into overdrive. The hell with it. He found the zipper at the back of her dress, slid it down and yanked the expensive material so it fell off her shoulders and pooled around her ankles. Ankles still supported by those sexy high heels. She grabbed his shirt to pull him back to her and then ripped it open. Buttons and studs popped, and Niko had one moment of regret. He only had one tux shirt. Keeping his arms around her, he unfastened the cuff links and let the shirt join her dress on the floor.

"Bdrm," Lesley mumbled in the brief second she

detached her lips from his.

They walk-stripped their way there. Beneath the dress, Lesley wore a strapless black bra and black bikini panties. She made him think of a Victoria's Secret model. With smaller curves. But the curves she did have were doing it for him.

He backed her up to the bed. She sank down on it and furiously undid the button on his slacks, pulled the zipper down and tugged enough so they fell. From the back of her throat came the sexiest sound Niko had ever heard a woman make, before she pulled his boxers off as well. He almost came the moment she took him in her mouth. He hadn't expected this, not from her that was for sure. *Lesley* and *blowjob* were two concepts he'd have never put together, even in his fantasies. He wondered what else lurked under her reserved surface.

He hadn't been with a woman in a while. He needed to slow this thing down because it was getting out of control. When he couldn't stand it any longer, he eased away from her. "Okay. Okay."

She looked up at him, and Niko saw something in her eyes he'd never expected to see. Fear. Not of him exactly. Maybe she feared his rejection of her. "Not a chance," he whispered. He came down on top of her and kissed her, marveling at the silk of her hair against his fingers, the fire beneath her skin.

He ran his hands and his lips all over her, enjoying her response to his touch. Her pulse leaped in her throat. She gave a tiny sound of delight when his tongue touched her behind her ear. She tried to hurry him, to get him to do more, but speed was not his style, never had been. She might have started this seduction, but he was going to finish it. His way.

After a bit, he unsnapped her bra. She wasn't overly endowed, but what she did have was perfection. Her breasts were full and round like oversize peaches, each topped with a dusky pink areola. He brushed a fingertip against one. She sucked in a breath. He glanced up to see her watching him expectantly through slitted eyes. He smiled before lowering his mouth to suckle her. She liked that, if her long *aaah* of satisfaction was anything to judge by. He offered the same treatment to her other breast, keeping the first one occupied with his hand so it didn't get lonely.

Lesley moved restlessly beneath him, her thighs and silky panties brushing against his cock. He took a handful of silk and tugged the panties down until they got tangled in high heels. Lesley maneuvered herself up toward the pillows, which left Niko kneeling at the end of the bed. He picked up one of her feet and slid the shoe off to kiss her instep. She stared at him. He tossed the shoe aside. Niko eased the panties over her foot and then repeated the move. Lesley Robinson was now naked in his bed, and she was something. Long limbs and perfect skin. Lips swollen, hair tangled, nipples erect.

He tugged her legs apart and bent her knees.

"Nnnooo." Her half-assed objection meant less than nothing. She'd had her mouth on him. Turnabout was only fair play.

She had a neatly trimmed, sweet little bush. He found her easily with his tongue, hot, ready, and wet from their foreplay. He used his fingers on her, figuring she'd need more coaxing than she actually did. She came fast and hard, and Niko decided he really, really liked her.

He kissed his way back up to her lips, stopping long enough to enjoy her breasts once more. He trapped her, his cock beyond ready, cradled between her thighs.

"You sure about this?" he asked, brushing a strand of hair away from her face.

"I'm sure."

Niko hardly had to move to reach into the nightstand drawer for a condom.

"You don't need that," Lesley told him. "I took precautions."

I bet you did. "I like to take my own precautions," Niko assured her. It was the truth and a lie. He'd like nothing better than to have no barriers between them. But he also knew the painful consequences of what happened when he wasn't careful.

All systems go, he lay down next to her and pulled her close. He kissed her. Not like before, when they were almost battling each other, but tenderly and sweetly. Niko didn't want to fight. He'd shown her who was boss in the bedroom, so he could cede control back to her now. In seconds, the sweet tenderness turned to carnal sensuality. Lesley opened herself to him and he plunged inside. She was hot and tight on the inside, demanding and wild outside. Her teeth nipped at his skin while her nails raked his back and dug into his buttocks. He'd thought he could let her take control while holding on to his, but her every movement pushed him closer to the edge.

Finally, he trapped her hands with his, lacing his fingers through hers. Her eyes lit up as he plunged into her with long, sure strokes. She fought his hold but he wouldn't let go, so she fought him with the rest of her body, arching up, hiking her legs higher, and in some odd way she won. He couldn't hold out any longer, thrusting until he was drained. He collapsed on top of her before slowly rolling to her side. "*Madre de Dios.*"

"What does that mean?"

"It means you should come with a warning label."

"Hmppf." Lesley turned on her side and scooted away from him.

Niko chuckled. He rid himself of the condom and spooned her from behind, wrapping an arm around her waist. "It means you are one hot mama, chica."

****

Lesley smiled as she closed her eyes. For the first time in a long time, she'd gotten what she wanted. When she woke, it was to find herself surrounded by Niko's warmth. His arm still cradled her from behind but something hard and metallic pressed against her midriff. His watch. She smiled at the thought he hadn't taken it off. She lifted his wrist and looked at the time. Nearly three o'clock. She sighed. She'd have to leave soon. Which was exactly what she'd planned to do. Except now she didn't want to.

She'd expected, when she'd invited herself in, a quick, satisfying coupling, something base and animal. It had been ages since she'd been with anyone and longer than that since she'd felt any real desire or attraction. She figured she'd sleep with Niko Morales and get it out of her system. Nothing would change.

Niko, however, had other ideas. For what they'd shared had been more, much more, than the wham-bam-thank-you-sir she'd anticipated. He made love to her. She'd let him. If she was truly honest with herself, she'd wanted him to. She was a fool. Because that made it harder to forget, harder to walk away.

His arm tightened around her. He pulled her closer. His lips touched her shoulder, kissing her, at the same time his hand began stroking her in long, sweeping motions. From her waist, over the curve of her hip to her thigh and back. To her tummy, along her arm. It felt wonderful, but she made a sound of protest. She needed to find her clothes, get dressed and go home.

He had tattoos. A black one that reminded her of barbed wire encircled his left bicep. There was another one that looked like initials and a date she couldn't read over his heart. She wondered if there were more she couldn't see and made a mental note to ask him about them sometime.

Niko pressed her onto her back and half covered her with his body. "Why do you make those sounds? Like you want to object when we both know you're not going to?"

He looked at her, his fingers idly twisting through her hair, his cock pressed against her hip.

"I should go."

"Why?"

"Because I..." *Because I don't want anyone to know I slept with you.* Her answer trailed away. The truth would hurt him.

"You don't want to leave." He kissed her. She gave herself up to the heat of his mouth.

She didn't want the lovemaking this time. What she wanted was a good fuck her way. She got on top and had him inside her before he could stop her. His fingers dug into her hips. "What are you doing? Let me get a condom."

"I told you, you don't need one." She flexed her muscles around him and moved against him, reaching around to cup his balls and press her thumb against the base of his shaft.

He went rigid, arching up against her.

"Trust me, Niko. Do I seem like the kind of woman to do something stupid?"

She rode him then, letting him show her what he liked, what he needed. When it was over, she collapsed on top of him. The words she'd spoken echoed in her head. She was afraid she had done something terribly stupid. She'd fallen in love with Niko Morales.

Chapter Twelve

Niko edged his car through the gates of the Robinson estate to see Ricky, Lesley, and Mitch waiting for him on the front steps. Lesley wore running clothes: snug Spandex shorts and a matching top with a pair of running shoes covered in shades of neon pink, purple, and green. Her hair was pulled back into a high ponytail. Sunglasses covered her eyes.

He'd seen various versions of her—the business attire, the more casual weekend look she'd worn to the park, and now this athletic persona.

Niko parked behind Mitch's SUV, and when he got out, Ricky raced over, grabbed his hand, and led him back to the group.

"Good morning," he said to Lesley and Mitch, who returned the greeting. Niko looked at Ricky. "Ready to do some fishing, buddy?"

"Ready!"

Lesley smiled. "He's been ready since last night. I'm surprised he got any sleep at all."

"I slept," Ricky assured her. "I'm ready."

"Let's go then," Mitch said. He took his keys from his pocket and went to the driver's door. He opened the rear passenger door before he got in. "You're in the back, Ricky."

Ricky let go of Niko's hand and got settled in the car.

Niko had been looking forward to the Sheriff's Sun and Fun Day as well, an annual event that welcomed all school-age children from across the county. It was headquartered at the city pier, where volunteers organized fishing tournaments, a canoe race, and a sandcastle contest. There were prizes and games and free food. Carp's mother was dropping him off to meet them there.

Niko was in no hurry to leave. He liked this version of Lesley. He wouldn't mind standing here and looking at her all day. Or going for a run on the beach with her.

"Thanks for inviting him today. I think it's good for him to be one of the guys, you know?" Lesley said.

"I agree." Niko couldn't think of anything else to say.

"I'm going for a run," she said. "On the beach."

"Oh, yeah?"

"I should tell Ricky good-bye." She passed him, and he fell into step behind her. The running shorts outlined the perfect mounds of her bottom, which were as firm and taut as the rest of her. He remembered what they felt like cupped in his hands.

Lesley kissed Ricky, reminding him to behave himself and to have a good time. She said good-bye to Mitch before she added, "Bye, Niko."

"Bye." He stared after her until she disappeared around the corner of the house.

He got into the passenger seat and buckled his seat belt. Mitch stared at Niko.

"What?" Niko asked.

Mitch looked pointedly in the rearview mirror. "Nothing," he said with a grin. "Nothing at all."

The driveway gates closed behind them, and Niko

automatically glanced in the side mirror. A car parked on the shoulder just past the Robinson grounds fell in behind them. Normally cars weren't parked along the road, which was a simple two-lane with no sidewalk and no parking spaces. The only vehicles he ever noticed parked outside the properties were service vehicles like those belonging to landscapers or cable companies.

Niko spent much of his youth watching Carlos' back, because even as a kid he was a reckless hothead who fell into a lot of trouble with little effort. Niko learned to be vigilant, to keep an eye out for anyone looking to do some damage to Carlos. It became second nature for him to be aware of his surroundings, of anything out of the ordinary.

That car was something out of the ordinary.

If Mitch noticed, he didn't comment. Ricky kept up a constant patter of conversation from the backseat, asking questions and offering tidbits of information about his previous trips to the pier, one in particular where he watched a brown pelican swallow a fish right in front of him.

The car followed them all the way to the parking area for the pier before Niko lost sight of it. The only things he knew for sure were that it was an older model compact and a woman with long dark hair drove.

They made their way along the pier, Mitch and Niko stopping to greet fellow officers, until they found an open space along the railing. Mitch baited the hook for Ricky, showing him how it was done and promising to let him do it next time.

Niko let Mitch take charge of getting Ricky's line in the water while he scanned the crowded pier. After his conversation with Lesley about her former housekeeper's visit, after he'd seen the picture she'd left, he'd had an uncomfortable feeling about the woman. It took a lot of chutzpah to barge into someone's home, especially one like the Robinsons', make demands and attempt to see a member of the family who was off-limits.

Niko pulled the cap he wore down on his head, using it and his sunglasses to fight the glare coming off the water. Kids and adults lined the pier railing, and the din of conversation and excited squeals when a fish was pulled out of the water added to the festive feel of the day. The scents of hot dogs cooking over an open flame and popcorn popping wafted on the warm air.

Along the beach below, the sandcastle contest was in full swing. Kids of all ages darted to and fro with buckets of sand and seawater, well supervised by adults. The canoes were up at a pass about a quarter mile away from the pier rather than on the open water. But all Ricky wanted to do was fish, and Niko couldn't blame him. The kid lived on the beach, and he could build a sandcastle anytime he wanted.

He saw no one resembling the woman from the car. It seemed like three-quarters of the sheriff's department had come out today to help with the event. Most of the chaperones were male.

"I got one! I got one!" Ricky yelled.

Niko turned back in time to see something tugging on Ricky's line.

"Okay," Mitch said. "Give it a tug." He put his hand on Ricky's fishing rod and demonstrated. "Gotta get him hooked. Uh-oh. Okay, reel it in. Like this." He showed Ricky how to work the reel.

The hook dangled emptily on the end of the line. "Where's my fish?" Ricky looked worriedly up at Mitch.

"He got away," Mitch replied. "It's okay. Sometimes you get a smart fish who takes the bait and gets away. You want to bait the hook this time?"

"Yeah!" Ricky's moment of disappointment disappeared as he switched his attention to the small bucket of bait Mitch set near the rail.

While Mitch instructed Ricky to lean in and grab one of the bait fish, Niko turned back to the crowd. Still he saw no one suspicious. He leaned on the rail next to Ricky and watched his line drop into the water a second time. He didn't quite see the point, especially since today's event was strictly catch and release. But Ricky was having a blast.

Mitch should have had children, Niko decided, watching the older man instruct and encourage Ricky. He was a natural. Niko wondered how he himself would have been as a father. In his younger years, he hadn't had much to offer a woman or a child. Maybe in the future though, he'd have that opportunity. The maturity, the financial stability, a lifetime relationship with someone who wanted the same things he did.

No matter how hard he tried to steer them away, his thoughts turned back to Lesley. That, he warned himself once again, was never going to happen. The idea that cool, wealthy, always-in-control Lesley Robinson would ever deign to become seriously involved with a former gang member was laughable.

All his life, he'd seen what he couldn't have, what others told him he'd never have. No one expected him to escape the way of life he'd pursued into young adulthood. Even he hadn't seen a way out until he'd been forced to make the toughest choice ever. He'd turned on his boyhood friend in order to save the life of an innocent child: his own child.

He'd sent Carlos, who had been like a brother to him, to prison. And now someone else was raising his son. He'd walked away from the life he'd been living and made himself concentrate on creating a different life, a better life. Then came the idea for the community center. If he got out, so could others like him if someone showed them the way. Who better to do so than someone who'd walked the same path?

"*Buenos días.*"

While Niko had been ruminating while staring out at the gulf, he hadn't noticed the woman who'd taken a position along the railing next to him.

He turned to look at her. She'd pushed her sunglasses up to hold back her long dark hair and clutched an oversize shoulder bag at her side. A colorful top stretched snugly across an impressive bustline, and lime-green capris outlined her curves from the waist down.

Niko returned the greeting, taking a moment to study her. The hairs on the back of his neck stood up. This was the woman from the car. She bore a strong resemblance to the woman in Lesley's picture. He turned sideways so his body blocked Ricky, who still waited for a bite on his line. Mitch leaned against the railing on the other side of Ricky. Between the two of them, no way was this woman getting close to the boy, if that was her intention.

"A beautiful day," she said, never taking her gaze off Niko. "You are here with your son?" She tilted her head to indicate Ricky behind him.

"No. A friend. Want to take a walk?"

She thought for a moment before she said, "Okay."

Niko took her arm and began to escort her down the pier, back toward the entrance and the parking lot. "I know who you are," he said. "You have no business here." He smiled at a couple of the deputies they passed, lifted his chin in acknowledgment of a couple of others.

Maria jerked her arm out of his grasp. "It is a free country. I can go where I want."

He wrapped his fingers around her elbow. "Don't make a scene," he growled. "Or I'll have you arrested."

"For what?" she huffed. "I do nothing wrong."

"Yet." Niko hustled her past the crowd to a relatively quiet area just beyond the boardwalk entrance. He released his hold on her and stared her down, memorizing her features in case he saw her lurking about again. "What do you want?"

"This is not your business." She glanced over his shoulder before looking at him again. "I not have to tell you anything."

"Maybe I can help you."

She gave him a distrustful look before her gaze swept back up the pier they'd just left. "I do not think so." Her words were sad, wistful.

Niko fought the pang of sympathy he felt, reminding himself that she must be pretty tough and calculating to approach Lesley in her own home. "Consider this a warning then. Stay away from Ricky. Stay away from Lesley."

"Who are you?" Her voice shook. "Who are you to tell me what I can do? You are no one to me!" She shouted, drawing attention from a couple of late arrivals making their way toward the pier. "You cannot arrest me for nothing. You do not threaten me with nothing!" She dug into her purse for her car keys. "The Robinsons owe me. They will pay. You tell *that* to Miss Lesley."

When she went to jab the keys toward Niko's face, he grabbed her wrist. "Leave now," he said keeping his voice low. "Or I'll arrest you for assaulting a law enforcement officer."

She yanked her wrist away and stumbled backward. With one last glare, she stomped off on the silly high-heeled sandals. Niko watched her disappear into the parking lot, thinking he'd gotten at least one clue about her. He'd noticed an ID card attached to her key ring. Apparently she worked at the Willow Bay Beach Club Hotel.

"Niko!" Carp sprinted toward him, his head half turned to watch Maria's retreat. "Everything okay?" He skidded to a stop, his gaze following Niko's until Maria disappeared between cars in the parking lot.

"Yeah. It's fine."

"Was that...? It looked like the woman from the park."

"Did it?" Niko tried to keep his tone light.

"Is she after Ricky?"

"What makes you say that?"

Carp shrugged. "I don't know. Ricky's here, isn't he? He was at the park that day. That's who she wanted to talk to."

Niko turned and they started walking along the pier. "Yeah, he's here, but I honestly don't know what it is she wants. You keep an eye out, okay? I'd rather she didn't come anywhere near him."

"I'm on it," Carp said seriously.

Niko smiled behind Carp's back. He had to hand it to Carp's mother. She'd raised a smart, polite, hardworking boy. The kid had the makings of greatness. He'd be a helluva man one day as long as he didn't lose his way. It was kids like this Niko wanted to fight for.

Chapter Thirteen

In the darkness of her bedroom, Lesley stared at the ceiling, fighting a war she knew she was going to lose. Truth: a war she *wanted* to lose.

With one decisive move, she flipped the covers back, left the bed, and crossed to her walk-in closet. She donned a light cotton shift dress and sandals and let herself out the side door of her suite, one with an alarm code all its own that wasn't connected to the main system. She'd purposely left her car parked under the porte cochere instead of in the garage.

Anticipation and excitement thrummed inside her as she steered the Lexus to the end of the drive and through the gates. Thirteen minutes later she parked behind Niko's car. His street was quiet and dark except for the streetlamps at either end of the block and a few shaded windows with light glowing behind them. Her dashboard clock read one fifteen.

She locked the car, the beep of the alarm seeming extra loud in the quiet night. At his door, she knocked firmly, feeling almost sick with nerves. A couple of minutes passed before she saw movement in the side panel. The deadbolt turned. The moment the door opened she went for him, shoving the door closed behind her. She barely heard him flip the deadbolt home.

She plastered herself against him, every sense she

possessed coming alive at once. Niko guided her back to the bedroom while they kissed. By the time they reached the bed, he'd slid the zipper of her dress all the way down, and a slight tug sent it to the floor.

She hadn't bothered with a bra and her sandals were easily toed off. Niko wore only a pair of cotton boxers, which made them exactly even. In her excitement Lesley almost forgot to breathe. All she knew was she needed Niko right now, and he obliged her, fucking her hard and fast.

Exactly the way she wanted.

****

Afterward, they lay next to each other, both panting. The ceiling fan whirred overhead in lazy circles, doing little to cool the heat they'd created. She waited for the crash of regret to wash over her, but it didn't come. This was the third time she'd done this, shown up at his home in the dead of night. He hadn't turned her away, hadn't asked why she was there. She came at him as soon as he opened the door, and he responded.

She needed sex. That's what she told herself. Sex with a man she liked. Sex with a man she was attracted to. Sex with a man who kept it simple, who didn't ask questions, who could be discreet.

Lesley smiled to herself thinking how lucky she'd been to find Niko. That he'd been so willing to serve not only as her escort, but also welcomed her into his bed.

Without a word, he got up and left the room. A few minutes later she heard the whir of the refrigerator and ice plinking into a glass, then another, lower hum of water from the same source. Niko returned with the glass. He drank some, then offered the rest to her.

"Thanks," she whispered, sipping some and giving the glass back to him.

He set it on the nightstand and lay next to her without touching her. He tucked his hands under his head and stared at the ceiling. Lesley frowned. This was not normal Niko behavior. Usually after the first quick go-round and a brief resting period, he began what she'd come to think of as his lovemaking ritual. Lots of stroking exploration, lots of skin-to-skin contact and mouth-to-skin contact while they both got worked up again.

Something was different tonight., A weird kind of tension settled in the air between them. Lesley didn't like it. The bedside clock told her it was nearly two. In about another hour, hour and a half max, she needed to leave. The very last thing she wanted was for anyone to discover where she went or what she did when she left the house in the middle of the night.

Her visits to Niko were her secret. And his, she supposed. She'd never expressly told him to keep it a secret. She'd simply assumed he would. Did she need to ensure his continued silence?

She slid across the narrow space between them and pressed herself against his side. She did what he usually did to her. Caressed his chest, across the flat abs and along his side, the tops of his thighs. She still hadn't asked about his tattoos, but she was in no mood for conversation. He stirred, but she avoided direct contact with his cock. She angled her head under his arm and kissed his throat, his neck, just under his ear, sinking her teeth into his earlobe and tugging.

His arms came around her, and he kissed her

deeply, their tongues fighting a war of their own. The tension between them Lesley had sensed earlier dissolved. They made love in the real sense of the words, giving and taking until they were both sated. She felt as though her bones were melting into the bed as she lay close to him, his arm and one of his legs flung across her.

She didn't want to leave. She never wanted to leave. Each time she was in his bed, the last thing she wanted to do was get dressed and go home. But she had no choice. She wiggled out from under his limbs, smiling when he squeezed her thigh before he let her go.

In the dark, she found her panties and her dress and put them on. Then her sandals. She bent over the bed and kissed Niko's temple. She didn't know if he was still awake or not. She sighed, fighting the same war with herself again, wishing with all her heart she could get back into bed with him and stay there until morning.

On tiptoe she made her way down the hall, released the deadbolt and closed the door quietly behind her.

****

Three hours later, Niko opened one eye to glare at his alarm clock, as if that would be enough to stop its insistent beeping. No such luck. He reached out and slammed the snooze button with an open palm, sank back into his pillow and closed his eyes.

The last thing he wanted to do was get up, get dressed and report for his eight o'clock shift. Lesley's visit robbed him of much needed sleep and left him pleasantly exhausted.

At the same time, he wasn't entirely pleased with the turn their relationship had taken. She seemed to think after the first time she could show up whenever she chose and be serviced by him. Of course she thought so because that's exactly what he'd been doing.

What was he supposed to do, he asked himself, rearranging his pillow and turning his back on his alarm clock. It wasn't like he didn't want to have sex with Lesley Robinson. He just hadn't thought it would happen and certainly not the way it did, with her on the offensive like that. He'd never have made a move on her. Would he? Probably not. She was out of his league, and they both knew it. A thought that hadn't rankled before, but it sure did now.

He pounded a fist against the mattress in frustration. He'd never be on equal footing with Lesley. He could allow her to use him, he supposed, or he could stand up to her and tell her in no uncertain terms that he wasn't going to be her stud horse any more. He should have said something to her last night. He'd been going to, but then she'd sidled up next to him and touched him, kissed him, the heat of her naked body sending signals he couldn't ignore. Afterward he didn't have the energy. He didn't want to spoil the mood their lovemaking created.

But soon, he decided, he'd have to lay it on the line with Lesley. He was pretty sure she wasn't going to like it. But then, he reminded himself as he turned off the alarm clock and got out of bed, neither would he.

Chapter Fourteen

Lesley looked at the phone while it rang. She'd been ready to call it a day, ready to sneak out a little early, have a glass of wine before dinner. Try to unwind. The calls she didn't answer would be forwarded to the small downtown office. She glanced at her watch. Probably the staff there had already left for the day, and the caller would get a recorded message asking to try again during normal business hours. Against her better judgment, she pressed the button for line one and picked up. "Lesley Robinson."

"Lesley. Hi. I'm glad I caught you."

"Who is this?"

"It's—it's Steven."

Lesley didn't want to think about what it meant that she didn't recognize the voice of a man she'd once loved, a man she'd thought she'd spend the rest of her life with. "What do you want?"

"I need to talk to you. I thought we could get together. Have a drink or something."

"I have nothing to say to you and no desire to have a drink with you. If that's all—"

"It's about Maria."

There weren't too many things Steven could have said to stop her cold, but Maria was one of them. She strove to keep her tone neutral and only mildly curious. "What about her?"

"She's been to see me."

Lesley waited.

"She's made threats."

"What kind of threats?"

"I'd rather not discuss it over the phone. Meet me at McCabe's in half an hour."

"Steven, I don't want to—" He'd hung up.

Lesley stared at the receiver in her hand. "Dammit."

Just like Steven to leave her hanging, feeling like he'd got the upper hand. Apparently, Maria wasn't going to give up on whatever it was she'd come back for. The woman was going to make her life miserable just as she had six years ago.

****

Lesley paused inside the door to McCabe's Irish Pub. It was downtown, next to a gourmet seafood restaurant. Its outdoor seating area looked over the courtyard in front of the Willow Bay Playhouse. The pub itself was nothing special, but it catered to a certain clientele, mostly young executives who spent their days staring at contracts or managing trust funds and who wanted a cold beer and a big-screen television tuned to any sport playing at the moment.

She located Steven in a booth near the back. He'd already ordered a beer. Lesley made her way to him and slid into the seat across from him. He half rose from his seat as she sat down. Why did he bother, she wondered, pretending to have respect for her. He'd walked all over her, and she'd thrown him out of her life. Why couldn't he just stay there?

"What would you like?" he asked as a young female server in a tight green T-shirt with the

McCabe's logo approached.

"Perrier with lime, please."

Lesley faced Steven. He looked away first, feigning interest in the soccer match on the screen behind the bar. After her drink arrived and the server left, she poured the water into the glass and took a sip, enjoying the crisp, refreshing bubbles.

Steven began, "You knew she was back."

"Yes."

He turned his beer glass round and round on the square coaster. "She came to see me a couple of months ago with this cockamamie story about your dad."

"What story?"

"That he's her father."

Lesley tried not to let her surprise show. She'd spent years learning to school her features into a calm mask, never to let anyone see what she thought or felt. She used it at everything from board meetings to business dinners and wasn't about to let it slip in front of her ex-husband.

"Go on."

"I told her it was bullshit, and even it were true, which I don't think for one minute that it is, she'd never be able to prove it. I told her you'd never allow her to get close enough to Richard to prove it."

So that's why she wanted to see my father. That's why she left that picture with me.

"You're right about that," she said and took another sip of water.

"She asked for my help."

Lesley narrowed her eyes at him. "How does she think you can help her?"

"God knows. Because I'm a lawyer? Maybe she

thinks I'd want to help her because of our past? She offered to share whatever she got with me."

"Whatever she got? From my family, you mean? I hope you told her what she'd be sharing with you is half of nothing."

"Basically, yes, that's what I told her. But she keeps coming around, pushing, prodding, insisting she's Richard's daughter—and as such she's owed her share of the family's fortune."

Lesley sat back, pretending to be relaxed. "But as you said, she'd have to prove it first."

Steven took a sip of his beer and contemplated the tabletop for several moments before he said, "She threatened me."

"How did she do that, pray tell?"

Steven glanced around, and Lesley noticed the after-work crowd had grown substantially since they'd been talking. There were no longer empty seats around the bar and those still vying for service were congregated between the bar and the booths. The noise level had doubled, and the bartenders and servers were all scrambling to keep up with demand.

Lesley shivered, her sleeveless dress no match for the frigid air pumping out of the vent behind their table.

Steven leaned forward, having no desire to be overheard.

"Threatened to come forward, go to the press, tell them about our aff—about what happened. About the kid. Look, I've only just gotten back on track with my life. I don't need this."

"She wants to create a scandal, and she hopes we'll pay her off to prevent it."

"Something like that. She named a price."

"How much?"

"Half a million."

Lesley felt like she'd been punched in the stomach. She tried to think quickly. Maria had not made overt threats during her visit. She hadn't demanded anything except to see Richard. She'd only insinuated she was owed something. When that failed, she went to Steven to enlist his help in obtaining that something, and when he wouldn't help her, she'd named a price for her silence.

She considered everything at stake. Mostly her family's reputation. But even more than that. Her father's good name. Ricky would be adversely affected. She could envision the ranks of the Royal Cove Club closing against her, shunning her, her mother, her son. The things Maria said might not be true, at least about who her father was. But even if all she did was make her affair with Steven public, and acknowledge herself as Ricky's biological mother, it would be enough.

The public facade Lesley had nurtured and protected all these years would crumble like dust. If she didn't prove Maria Delgado wrong, everyone would think there was something to her story. Twenty-five or fifty years from now, some matriarch from another Willow Bay family would begin the story with, "Rumor had it that Richard Robinson had an illegitimate daughter…" and it would go on from there.

"Why did you ask to see me, Steven?"

"I think you should consider DNA testing—"

"Absolutely not! My father is not her father. I will not sink to her level."

"You don't know that. You don't know what your father is capable of. Or was capable of. I cheated on you right under your nose, and you didn't know."

Lesley's fists clenched so hard her fingernails dug into her palms. How she longed to give Steven what he deserved. The kind of punch that would wipe that condescending smirk off his face once and for all. "Don't you dare compare yourself to my father," Lesley warned, emotion tightening her throat. "He is and always was an honorable man. He loves my mother and would never—"

"He's a man." Steven sat back, his expression stony. "Ask a hundred men if they thought they could get away with it, would they cheat? A hundred of them will say yes. If Richard Robinson was out of the country, away from your mother, and the opportunity is there, as I'm sure it was, you don't know he didn't take advantage of it."

"My father is not the type of man who takes advantage—of things or people. Unless you've got something else to say, I think we're done here." Lesley moved to the end of the booth.

"She can ruin me," Steven said, and something in his tone stopped Lesley. She looked across the table at the man she'd once loved, the man she'd pledged herself to. He was a stranger to her now. Maybe he always had been and she'd fooled herself into seeing what she wanted to see, believing the lies he'd fed her.

Was it even remotely possible that her father did the same thing to Maria's mother? If that was true, the man who'd taught her everything she knew, who'd loved her, who'd been proud of her, was a fraud. If Richard wasn't who she thought he was, that meant she wasn't who she thought she was either.

Her judgment about Steven had been impaired.

Was her judgment about her father also faulty? What about Niko? Was she wrong about him too? What if she once again chose unwisely?

"I'm sorry if that's true, Steven, but I can't help you."

"The hell you can't. You can but you won't."

"Fine. I won't. I don't owe you anything. You and Maria made your beds, so lie in them. The way I see it, you two deserve each other."

"She can ruin you too," he insisted.

"No. What she can do is create some smoke. I'm willing to pit my family's reputation against her scheming if it comes to that. You know this town. It runs on gossip and innuendo and supposition. Maria will be made out to be a disgruntled employee with a grudge, nothing more. We can weather whatever she brings on. I protect what's mine. I won't let her hurt anyone I love."

"And since I'm no longer part of your circle, you'll hang me out to dry."

"I'm done cleaning up your messes. As far as I'm concerned, you can go to hell. Take Maria with you."

Lesley fast-tracked her way to the door and shoved it open, nearly knocking over two patrons about to enter. By the time she reached her car, she was breathing hard and her hands were shaking. She pushed the start button and let the car's air-conditioning wash over her while she tried to control her breathing, to settle her careening thoughts.

In her head she heard her father's voice reminding her of one of his favorite quotes. *The road to hell, having been paved with good intentions, is now ready for travel.*

She'd tried to do right by Maria, by Ricky, by her family, even by Steven. She'd kept their secrets, kept them safe, protected them. But at what expense?

Chapter Fifteen

Lesley parked her car and walked the familiar path to Niko's front door. It was dark out, and the streetlamps had only just flickered to life. She knocked and waited, but there was no answer. His car sat in the driveway, but it seemed he wasn't home. She knocked again, fighting her sense of disappointment, willing him to be there.

"Lesley."

She turned quickly and flattened herself against the stucco, pressing a hand to her chest. "Niko." Relief made her voice breathy. A tiny nervous laugh escaped her. "You scared the life out of me." She took a step toward him. "What are you doing out here?"

"Waiting for you."

"Oh. Well, here I am."

He held out his hand. "Come with me."

Lesley stepped forward and took it. "Aren't we going inside?"

"We'll see."

He led her around the side of the house, through the damp grass. Water droplets dripped off a bottlebrush tree. Frogs were in the middle of a round of croaking choruses.

Niko opened a screened door for Lesley. She stepped inside and stopped. "Oh."

****

Niko tried to see the space through her eyes. Were the candles too much? The fountain tinkled gently in one corner. He nudged her forward.

"I didn't know this was here."

Of course you didn't. You never get past the bedroom.

"Have a seat."

She perched on the edge of one of the cushioned chairs.

"I made tea."

"Tea?"

"Yes. Tea." He poured some from the pot into small mugs and handed one to her. "Try it."

Lesley took a sip and set the mug back on the table. Niko held his mug in one hand and relaxed in his chair. He enjoyed throwing her off balance. He'd ceded too much control of their relationship, but that was about to change. Either that or this, whatever this was between them, would be over. He sipped the oriental green tea with hints of orange, and waited.

The CD he'd selected of simple instrumental melodies played softly in the background. He loved unwinding here, especially after one of the hard rains. He found the steady drip of water from the gutters and the trees, mingled with the frogs' voices, relaxing.

"What's this about?" she finally asked. She'd been watching him the entire time, probably trying to gauge his mood. He knew she wouldn't tiptoe around but would get straight to the point.

He lowered the mug. "I thought we could spend some time together. Talking. Getting to know each other."

"We already know each other."

155

"In bed."

"That's enough."

"Is it?"

"Isn't it?"

"Not for me."

"Oh." He didn't miss her sigh of disappointment.

Niko leaned forward. "I want more." Direct was the only way to go at this point.

"Oh." Now she sounded defeated.

"If you were looking for sex with somebody, no strings attached, you picked the wrong guy."

"Oh."

"Look, I like you."

Her gaze met his, but even in the candlelight he saw caution in her eyes. He plowed ahead. "I like everything about you. I like trying to figure out what makes you tick. But I'm not your toy. I'm not here to scratch your itch whenever you're in the mood. You don't want to pursue whatever this is we've got going, that's your choice. You know the way home."

"Wow." Her chin came up. "Police brutality."

He thought he saw a hint of a smile there. "Only when necessary."

"I never meant to...use you. I just...oh, this is so embarrassing."

"What? What's embarrassing?"

She shook her head, reached for her tea and took a sip. Her hand wasn't quite steady when she set it down. "We come from such different places," she said thoughtfully, glancing at him.

"We're both right here," he pointed out.

"I don't see how this can work."

"Maybe it won't," he conceded.

She sighed, giving in a little. "What did you want to talk about?"

"Anything. Everything. Pick a topic."

"It'd probably be better if you picked one."

"Okay then. Ricky. What's the story there?"

Lesley pressed back in her chair as if he'd slapped her. She stared at him, took a deep breath and let it out slowly. "If you want me to tell that story, I'll need something stronger than tea."

On impulse during his last food-shopping expedition, Niko bought a four-pack of individual servings of white wine. They were outrageously priced, though certainly not of the quality Lesley was used to. He'd stowed them in the refrigerator, annoyed with himself for thinking he'd ever have a reason to open even one of them. Lesley wasn't exactly high maintenance, but she was…expensive.

He and she might be worlds apart, but their worlds kept colliding. Like two spheres floating separately in the universe whose boundaries overlapped and interconnected. They moved closer and closer together until one fit perfectly into the other. After the explosion they went back to floating separately, each in its own distinct orbit—until inevitably they came together again.

Niko knew he was overthinking whatever this was with her, but he couldn't help the way he was wired. There was something there, something more than their agreed-upon quid pro quo, something more than sex. Lesley must think so too, or she would have turned around and left by now.

He returned with a glass of wine for her and a beer he didn't really want for himself. Lesley took a sip. She held the glass up and looked at it in the dim light. "Not bad. I'm surprised you have wine."

"I bought it for you."

Their gazes locked. Whatever she thought of his admission, she didn't comment on it. Instead she took another sip. It seemed to strengthen her resolve. "Six years ago, a little more than that now, I suppose, I was married to Steven. He was an assistant with the state attorney's office. I was learning to run my father's companies. We lived in a suite in my parents' home, along with the domestic staff included with it. Specifically, we had a maid. Maria.

"I traveled quite a bit with my father. It was always the plan that I would take over his position as CEO and he'd remain as chairman of the board for the Robinson Group. I had a lot to learn, and my father to show me the ropes. I loved it. I was happily married. Steven and I enjoyed our careers. We lived on the beach, were engaged in an active social life. We had it all," she added softly, sadly, before she drank some more wine.

"You know how they say bad things come in threes? That's what happened. Only it was more like three times three.

"I discovered Maria was pregnant about the same time my father suffered a massive stroke. I don't know how she hid her pregnancy or if I was just that unobservant. I missed what went on in my own house right under my nose." Lesley sighed and peered into her wineglass.

"My father was so ill. I was crazy with worry, but I had to step in and take his place in the company. I didn't have a choice. The baby came early and was born with heart problems. He needed surgery and treatment right away. Maria's work visa, however, had expired. The deportation process had already begun."

"They wouldn't make an exception? For a new mother with a sick baby?"

"You'd think they would, wouldn't you? I did what I could, but frankly I was overwhelmed. Her staying or going wasn't high on my list of priorities. She begged me to take care of a sick, helpless baby. I didn't know how to refuse. None of it was his fault. I felt sorry for her. She went back to El Salvador, and I kept Ricky."

"What about the father?"

Lesley swallowed a gulp of wine. She laughed bitterly. "Maria wouldn't tell me who the father was. I thought perhaps she didn't know. I didn't push it. When I told Steven what had happened, that I'd agreed to take custody of the baby, he went nuts. I'd never seen him behave like that before. That's when I knew."

"He's Ricky's father."

Lesley pointed a finger at Niko and drained the rest of her wine. She set the glass down.

"You got rid of Steven and kept Ricky."

"I didn't consciously plan to at the time. To keep Ricky, that is. Steven certainly didn't want him. Turns out Maria didn't either. At least not then. But I couldn't turn my back on him. I felt…responsible somehow."

"Want some more wine?" Niko asked.

"No. I should go." Lesley stood and so did Niko.

He slid his arms around her waist. "Don't go."

"You probably think I know what I'm doing, that I have it all under control. Everyone thinks that. The truth is, I'm a mess." She tried to smile. She put a finger over his lips. "Sshhh. Don't tell anyone."

He gazed into her eyes. "I think you're incredible."

He sifted her hair through his fingers.

"Niko, don't."

"Don't go." He bent and brushed his lips against hers.

"Niko." She sighed. He moved closer and she slid her hands down his chest.

"Don't go," he whispered again. His mouth moved along her jaw to that sensitive spot below her ear.

****

Her knees went weak. Every time Niko touched her like this, she came alive. Sometimes she felt like Sleeping Beauty the way she'd been living the past several years. Existing. Functioning. But not really feeling anything. Everything inside her had gone to sleep, held there by the brittle shell she'd created to keep it all together.

But Niko broke through the shell, and she'd caved so easily it astonished her. No one else had been interested or even tried to get past her flimsy defense system. She didn't know if he'd tried very hard either. With him it just happened. Instinctively she wanted to trust him. She wanted...she hadn't figured out what exactly she wanted from him yet. So she'd tried to keep it simple. Keep it sexual. Even though she knew there was more to it. Leave it to Niko to know it too and to push her to the next level.

Very few people knew what she'd just told him. There were whispers, certainly. Rumors and gossip at the time. Speculation. But the Robinsons circled the wagons. Steven knew better than to brag about his indiscretion. He needed to rebuild his reputation and save his career. Maria was of no consequence. Lita could be trusted, and Mitzi? Well, who knew whether

Mitzi shared confidences with some of her women friends? Lesley hoped not. She hoped her mother knew better.

Lesley had lost a husband and a housekeeper and gained a son. She threw herself into running the Robinson Group, overseeing her father's care, Ricky's care, her family's well-being. She'd lost part of herself along the way. She saw that now. But somehow, being with Niko like this made her feel whole again. Like she was reforming into the complete person she'd been before she fell into that Sleeping Beauty state six years ago.

"Are we done talking?" she whispered against Niko's ear. She let her fingertips run along the back of his head before she wrapped her arms around his neck. She loved the press of his body against hers, all muscle and man.

In answer he kissed her, a long, sensual kiss filled with gentleness and carnality. This was what she loved...loved?...she'd worry about that later—about Niko.

He maneuvered her through the house. Bits and pieces of their clothing came off along the way. Her panties were the last thing to go before she landed on the bed. Niko shucked his shorts and underwear and joined her.

Hands, mouths, tongues. They never stilled, touching each other everywhere until they were joined together. Everything seemed to go in slow motion. She hadn't come yet. Niko knew it. She was vaguely disappointed because his previous policy appeared to be "ladies first."

But this, this was driving her crazy. Not that she

wasn't enjoying it or participating. She sucked his tongue and angled her body against his. Excitement built, but oh, why were men and women created this way? There wasn't enough...friction...where she needed it to be. It wasn't direct enough...it wasn't... Oh, *whoa*.

Her thoughts went spinning in another direction when Niko ended their kiss. He pressed her knees out, away from his body, opening her to him. He slid against her in an entirely new way. She shivered in delight. It didn't take much before she arched against him and he sank back deeply inside her, swallowing her moans of ecstasy with a kiss.

Afterward they lay tangled together. Lesley dozed off briefly. Maybe Niko did too, but she was always aware of time marching along. The last thing she wanted to do was leave this bed. Put her clothes back on. Drive home. Pretend she'd been there all night and that it was just another normal day.

"Stop it." Niko's sleepy-sounding grumble startled her.

She hadn't moved. Hadn't made a sound. "What?"

He turned on his side and drew her into his embrace and spoke into her hair. "Stop thinking about what time it is."

"I can't help it."

He pulled back. She saw him looking at her in the dim light while he brushed the hair back from her face. "I can give you something else to think about." Then he rolled onto his back with her on top.

"Yes," she agreed, smiling at him. "You certainly can."

Chapter Sixteen

Lesley glanced through the stack of correspondence her assistant had dropped off. Each morning, Jessica efficiently sorted all the mail at the office, then brought anything requiring her personal attention to her immediately after her arrival.

Using her own sorting system, Lesley prioritized action items from those which only required reading. The last piece of paper she picked up was correspondence from a bank in Texas with an attached note from Jessica indicating that she'd done her best to resolve the issue herself, but the bank manager would speak only with Richard Robinson or someone authorized to act on his behalf.

Lesley frowned at the letterhead. As far as she knew, neither her father nor the Robinson Group had any dealings with Waco Community Bank & Trust, yet the letter addressed to Richard mentioned an account number. It was a mistake of some sort surely, but she decided the quickest way to get this piece of paper off her desk was to deal with it herself. She picked up the phone and dialed.

Ronald Ward took her call without delay. "Ms. Robinson. Thank you for calling."

"You're welcome. I believe there's been a mistake. To the best of my knowledge, neither my father nor our company has any business with your bank."

"Ah, yes. I see. Before we continue, may I ask, are you in fact authorized to speak on your father's behalf on personal matters?"

"I have a power of attorney, yes. I'm authorized to handle all of his affairs, both personal and business. I can email you a copy if you'd like."

"Yes, please." He rattled off his email address. Lesley brought up the document and sent it from her laptop.

"Got it," he said after a minute. "Everything looks to be in order. Could you, just as a precaution, give me your father's social security number and date of birth?"

Lesley rattled them off from memory. "Mr. Ward, I'm rather busy. I'd appreciate it if we could clear up this misunderstanding as quickly as possible."

"Of course, but there is no misunderstanding. Your father opened an account at our bank in June 1995."

"Are you certain?"

"Quite certain, yes."

"I'll check with our accountant, of course, but I don't recall seeing any bank statements for this account. I'm not aware of any deposits to it either."

"Oh, there haven't been any deposits since the original one when the account was opened," Ward said. "It's a non-interest-bearing account, so 1099s wouldn't be issued. All of the correspondence, was in fact handled by Mark Whitcomb, a local attorney. Sadly, he passed away last month, or I assume you'd have heard from him about this matter."

"I'm still not clear," she said. "Are you saying my father opened this account in 1995 and then simply left it in your hands and that of this local attorney?"

"Yes, well, I wasn't actually employed here in

1995. I came on board several years later, but I've reviewed the history of the account and your assessment is correct."

"I don't understand," Lesley continued, intrigued now. "What was the account for?"

"That I couldn't say," the banker answered. "All I can tell you is that on the first of every month, a transfer was made to a bank in El Salvador."

Lesley's mouth went dry. "Ex-excuse me. El Salvador, did you say?"

"That's correct."

"Do you happen to know who the money was transferred to? Was there a name on the account in El Salvador?"

"The name on the account was Elena Delgado."

"Delgado?" Lesley echoed in a strangled whisper.

"Correct. When the funds were depleted, I sent notice to Mr. Whitcomb asking if we should close the account."

"And?"

"Mr. Whitcomb didn't respond. I tried on more than one occasion to contact him without success before I learned of his passing. I made inquiries with the bank in El Salvador. The account there was closed, perhaps because no further transfers were made. I then had no recourse but to attempt to contact the owner of the account, your father, to determine his wishes."

Lesley remained silent while she tried to absorb what Ronald Ward had told her and what it meant. After a minute, he said, "Ms. Robinson? Are you still there?"

"Yes. I'm here. I don't know what to say. Could you tell me, by chance, the amount of the initial deposit into the account? And how much the monthly transfers were?"

"I have it right here." She heard the shuffle of papers before Ward spoke again. "The initial deposit was a hundred and fifty thousand dollars. The transfers were five hundred dollars a month."

"Over a period of twenty-five years."

"Yes. That is correct."

Propping her head in one hand, she struggled to absorb what all this meant. Her father had been funneling money to Maria's mother since Maria's infancy. Maybe even before that. Lesley could think of only one reason why he would do that.

"Shall I close the account then?" Ronald asked.

"Yes. Please do." *And let's never speak of this again.*

"I'll take care of it. Have a pleasant day."

"You too," Lesley replied automatically before she hung up.

A pleasant day? Not likely. The implications of what she'd learned in the past ten minutes churned around in her head. She didn't want to believe it was true.

Chapter Seventeen

"Hi, Daddy." Lesley bent and kissed her father's sunken cheek. He followed her with his eyes. The left side of his mouth lifted in a semblance of a smile. She smiled back. "How are you feeling today?"

The day nurse greeted Lesley while she finished situating Richard's computer in front of him. She gently put his glasses on and smoothed the hair over his ears. Although similar to the device created for Stephen Hawking, the hardware had been customized for her father's particular limitations. An infrared switch mounted on his spectacles caught the slightest of facial twitches to feed information into the computer about letter and word choices. After the nurse bustled away with an armful of sheets in need of laundering, Lesley took a seat near the hospital bed, where her father could see her easily and she had a good view of the computer's screen.

Lesley waited as Richard's efforts progressed across the screen to form two words. *Still kicking.*

It was his idea of a joke, and Lesley chuckled at his effort. The nursing staff kept him clean and comfortable. A physical therapist visited three times a week. He was fed a liquid diet. There was nothing wrong with his hearing. He read and watched television and movies. Without his computer, his communication skills were limited. A short email message could take him an hour to compose. Although he never gave up working on his memoir, he tired easily.

His health was precarious at best as he was prone to upper respiratory infections. Each year he weakened a bit more, grew thinner and sicker. Lesley pretended he hadn't changed a bit. She visited him twice a day, morning and evening. She kept him up-to-date on the business and chatted about family events. The weather. Anything and everything. She loved her father and looked up to him. She'd dreamed of running the Robinson Group with him at the helm for a good number of years, learning even more than he'd already taught her. When he retired, a date that should have been well in the future, she would take over for him as CEO.

But the stroke fast-tracked her into her father's position. It had taken her months to find her footing. The company not only survived but thrived under her leadership. She had her detractors of course, but she supposed she'd have them in any event.

"Daddy, I need to show you something and I need to ask you something, okay? It's important."

Richard kept his gaze on her.

"Do you remember Maria? The housekeeper who worked for Steven and me when we were married?"

After a simple prompt from Richard, a preprogrammed response appeared on the screen. *Yes.*

"She came here. To the house. She wanted to see you."

No.

Lesley wasn't certain if she imagined the worry lines that seemed to develop around her father's eyes. She smiled easily. "That's what I told her. But do you

168

know why she'd want to see you?"

No.

"You barely knew her if I recall."

Richard concentrated fiercely on Lesley's face.

"She gave me this. Have you seen it before?" Lesley held the photocopied picture up where her father could see it without straining.

No. Yes.

Lesley wasn't sure what to make of that. "You've seen it?" she asked carefully.

Yes.

"But it isn't the whole picture, is it?"

Richard stared hard at her. *No.*

"That's what I thought."

Lesley chose her next words carefully. "There was an account at a bank in Texas."

Yes.

"You set it up for Maria's mother."

Yes.

"Because you felt responsible for her."

A hesitation, then *Yes.*

Lesley couldn't take her gaze away. Her father stared at her with a burning intensity as if waiting for her to get to the question they both knew she had to ask. She didn't want to ask it. She didn't want to see another *yes* after she asked it, but she was sure that's what the answer would be.

Richard's gaze shifted to his computer. He began to create a message. Lesley didn't see the need. She wanted an answer. A simple yes or no.

She covered his hand with her own and squeezed, even though she knew he couldn't feel it. "Daddy, is Maria your daughter?"

Distracted from his writing, her father made a low growling sound in his throat. It managed to convey pain and agitation at the same time. Like a distress signal for someone with no other way to communicate. At the same time he began blinking so rapidly Lesley was afraid he was having a seizure.

The nurse appeared at Richard's side and spoke to him in soothing tones, blocking his view of Lesley with her upper body. Lesley had to let go of his hand. She felt as if she'd done something unforgivable. She stepped back out of Richard's line of sight while the nurse separated him from the computer, gently wiping at the tears pooled around his eyes.

Lesley stared at the few words her father had written, her eyes burning. She turned and left.

****

Niko stripped out of his uniform and headed straight for the shower. The uniforms were durable and practically wrinkle-proof, but whatever polyester blend they were made of did not breathe, and by the end of his shift, he was hot and uncomfortable, dying to rid himself of his work clothes.

Less than ten minutes later, he'd donned a pair of baggy madras shorts and a T-shirt and contemplated the limited contents of his refrigerator. An insistent knocking on his front door pulled him away from thoughts of dinner. He peeked through the sidelight to see Lesley. The moment he opened the door, she fell into him, grabbing on to him as though he were a life preserver in the middle of a hurricane-swept ocean.

He closed the door, returning her embrace, but alarm bells went off inside him. This was not the let's-go-to-bed-now Lesley embrace.

She didn't say anything, but he felt her tension, the lengths she went to hold everything in. Something was very, very wrong. "Did somebody die?" he whispered. It was the only thing he could think of. Her father perhaps.

She shook her head vigorously.

That was something, he supposed. He racked his brain for another reason she'd be so upset, so close to losing control.

Before he could think of one, a sob escaped from deep in her chest. With her head buried in his shoulder, she struggled to hang on to her emotions. "It's okay," he murmured. "Whatever it is, it'll be okay."

She grabbed fistfuls of his shirt as tears started to flow. He leaned back against the wall and held her, stroking her hair as he might a child's, occasionally murmuring calming reassurances.

Eventually she quieted, but she didn't move away. The refrigerator motor kicked on about the same time Niko's stomach growled. The mood shifted. Lesley made a sound he couldn't decipher and lifted her head, rubbing her fingers over the wet spot she'd made on his tee. She wouldn't meet his gaze.

He ducked his head to see her face. "Want something to drink?" he asked. "And a paper towel, maybe?

She gave him a watery chuckle and a wobbly smile.

Niko hooked an arm around her neck to keep her close and steered her into the kitchen. He handed her a paper towel from the roll on the counter and opened the refrigerator, popping the tops on two Corona Lights. "No limes," he informed her.

In the pantry he found a bag of tortilla chips and a jar of salsa. Alicia Sanchez would be scandalized. He set them on the counter and took the stool next to Lesley.

She sipped her beer. "Sorry about that." She nodded her head in the direction of the front door. More tears welled in her eyes. She dabbed at them with the paper towel. "Just for the record, I never cry."

"Never?"

"Rarely," she amended.

"Maybe you should do it more often."

"No. I despise women who are reduced to tears at the drop of a hat. It's weak."

"So what dropped?"

"My father."

"I thought you said—"

"While I was with him this morning, he had an episode which I'm afraid our conversation caused. But I found out something I didn't know. Something I didn't want to know."

She took another drink. Niko waited. "All the stuff I told you about Ricky? Steven's affair?"

Lesley sniffed and dabbed at her nose with the paper towel. Other than a slight redness around her nose and eyelids a little puffier than normal, she bore hardly any signs of her earlier breakdown. Every time her eyes filled with tears, she willed them away. "I think Ricky's mother is my half sister."

"Your think your father is…her father?"

"It looks that way, yes."

The look in her eyes, so full of pain, broke his heart. He couldn't even begin to imagine how she felt. "Come here." He drew her up and settled her on the sofa next to him, beers forgotten, while he pieced together what she hadn't yet told him. "What happened? Why do you think there's a connection between you?"

Lesley sniffed. "Because of the picture Maria left with me the first time she came to see me."

"Do you still have it?"

"Yes." She fumbled for her purse for the photo, then handed it to him.

"This is your father. And this supposedly is Maria's mother."

"There's a strong resemblance between them. I don't know why Maria would lie."

Niko raised an eyebrow but said nothing as he continued to study the photo. "So you think your father had an affair. With Maria's mother."

"Evidently."

"He had her deported? When she became pregnant?"

"I don't know exactly what happened."

"But your father knew? That she was pregnant?"

Lesley nodded and wiped away a tear from the corner of her eye. "It looks that way. He set up an account for her. That's how I found out. He set up an account with a bank in Texas twenty-five years ago. From there, regular transfers were made to a bank in El Salvador. My father must have known Maria was his daughter. He arranged for her to come here, to work in our home. But he couldn't acknowledge her as his daughter."

"Did she know? That he was her father?"

"I don't know. His stroke occurred almost at the same time everything blew up with Steven."

"He financially supported her, though. Along with her mother."

Lesley nodded. "Initially there was a lot of money in the bank account in Texas. A local attorney oversaw the transactions. There were no further deposits made to the account, so the balance dwindled until it was nothing."

"That's about the time Maria showed up here."

"Yes."

"It explains why she wanted to see your father. Why she wanted money."

"Yes."

Niko picked up the picture again and stared at it intensely, bringing it closer to his eyes. "This is a photocopy of an old photograph, and a not very good one at that."

"I know. But it's definitely my father. I'm as certain as I can be based on the resemblance that the woman is Maria's mother."

"I need a magnifying glass to be sure," Niko said, "but look here. It looks like someone's arm is around her. Whoever it belonged to was cut out of the picture."

Lesley studied the picture more closely. "I think you're right. This looks like part of an arm, here, and some of his hand is just barely visible there."

She glanced at Niko with hope in her eyes.

"In contrast, your father is sitting next to her, a few inches away. His hands are in his lap."

"You're right!"

"I think it's possible that whoever got cut out of the photo might be of some relevance. Perhaps your father was covering for him by supporting Maria and her mother all these years. Or maybe Maria's mother blackmailed your father."

"Maybe."

"Do you know where this picture was taken?"

"No."

"Your father's wearing a dress shirt. No tie and the sleeves are rolled up, but it looks like at some point during the day that picture was taken, he was dressed for the office."

Lesley continued to pore over the picture.

"Maybe there's a duplicate of this picture in your company archives. Or your mother might have seen it before. I think you should ask her."

Lesley groaned. "She's been through so much these past few years. I hate to bring it up and cause her more pain."

"Maybe she already knows. If she doesn't, well, she's family. Why should you go through this alone?"

"My father was always protective of her. I guess I've tried to follow in his footsteps."

"Your mother's probably a lot tougher than you give her credit for. Women tend to know when their husbands cheat on them."

"I don't want to believe my father's a cheat."

"Of course you don't. You don't want to hurt your mother, either. But what's the alternative? You leave the questions you have unanswered and you don't know what to think about your father? You deserve to know the truth one way or the other."

Lesley sniffed and dabbed at her nose. "I tried to ask Daddy about it earlier. He recognized the picture. He has a computer he uses to communicate, and he started to compose a message to me. It was taking so long and I was impatient, so I asked him if he was

Maria's father. He got so upset. It was horrible."

"Either he isn't Maria's father and what you've always believed about him is true. Or he is and you'll have to adjust your image of him. Maybe he made a mistake and then tried to do right after the fact. Or maybe the mistake wasn't on his part."

"The message he started? It said, 'Nothing else I could do.'"

"That's a pretty ambiguous statement, Lesley. Look, the easiest thing to do is ask your mother about it. If she can't help, then dig through the company archives for the original picture.

"I don't know. I don't even know how to ask her about it."

Niko ruminated for a moment, wondering how Mitzi would react to such a situation.

"The thing is," Lesley continued, her voice squeaky, "Maybe Ricky isn't my ex-husband's castoff that I agreed to take care of."

"Maybe he's your nephew."

Lesley dabbed at her eyes and nose again. "He's part of my family. He always has been. But I've been holding him at arm's length because I couldn't—I couldn't…"

Niko's arm tightened around her and he pressed his lips to her temple.

"I should have been a mother to him. Or at least a—a doting aunt. Instead, I've been…" Lesley tilted her head back against the sofa cushions. Tears leaked from her eyes and slid into her hair. "So cold. Efficient. I made sure he had everything he needed. Except someone who loved him."

Niko refused to offer a false argument in an

attempt to make her feel better. Most of what she said was true. Ricky had been a lonely little boy who instinctively knew he didn't exactly belong. "From what I've seen, you've changed that."

She just looked at him. "I've been trying. But I can't undo the way I've behaved toward him since the day he was born."

"No one gets to change the past. You just go forward and try to do better and be better every day."

"You remind me of that all the time," she said with a watery smile. "I saw the way you were with Ricky from the first time you met him. He didn't even know you, and he felt more comfortable around you than he did around me. Seeing the way you connected with him is what pushed me to confront myself about what I was doing."

He cleared his throat, wondering how this conversation got to be about him. "I was just being me. I like kids."

She offered another glimmer of a smile. "I know."

"Just keep doing what you're doing every day from now on. You and Ricky will be fine."

"I hope so, but I'm not sure…I'm not sure of anything at the moment."

"You're a smart woman. You'll figure it out."

"I might need to consult with someone with more experience."

"I'm available," Niko said. "But my fees are pretty high."

"That's okay," Lesley replied, moving in for a kiss. "Money's no object."

Chapter Eighteen

A few days later, after tormenting himself with whether or not to do it, Niko picked up the phone and called Lesley. He got right to the point. "I'm going to Sarasota this weekend to see some friends who are vacationing there. They have a boy about Ricky's age. Maybe the two of you would like to go with me?"

Prepared for an automatic rejection, he gripped the phone. He was nervous about visiting Hayley and Ray and Fletcher. Ever since they adopted his son, Hayley had kept Niko up to date on the boy's progress. She sent him pictures and wrote notes about how Fletcher was doing on a regular basis, but Niko hadn't seen them in four years. Fletcher was eight now, and he desperately wanted to see his son. He wanted to be certain he'd done the right thing in encouraging Hayley to adopt him. More than anything he wanted his son's childhood to be better than his. Which is why he'd bowed out of Fletcher's life early on—and stayed away for long periods of time.

"Sarasota!" Lesley exclaimed. "I haven't been there in ages."

"They're staying in a condo on Long Boat Key—"

"It's gorgeous there," Lesley interrupted.

"Is it? I've never been."

"When were you thinking of going?"

"Does that mean you'll go?" Niko wasn't sure

where he stood with Lesley or what the parameters of their relationship were. But after the night on the lanai, he'd thought they'd entered a new phase. Lesley had turned to him when she'd found out about her father's possible connection to Maria. She'd cried on his shoulder, poured out her heart to him. That meant something, didn't it?

He heard her shuffling papers, perhaps checking the calendar on her desk. "I wouldn't mind getting away for a day, and I don't see anything scheduled for the weekend. I can't think of any reason why we couldn't join you."

"Great. I'll pick you up Saturday morning around nine. Bring a swimsuit."

****

"Tell me about your friends," Lesley said once they were on their way. Ricky was installed in the backseat, engrossed in a movie, the buds of his iPad in his ears. Niko hadn't put up any objection when she'd suggested taking her car. Further proof, he chided himself, that he was under her spell. "How did you meet?"

Niko thought for a moment about how to explain his relationship with the Braddocks. "I knew Hayley when I lived in Jacksonville." That was the truth. "She met Ray after she relocated to a small town in northern Florida. They adopted a little boy. His name is Fletcher."

"You and Hayley…dated?"

He almost laughed out loud at the question. "No."

When he first met Hayley, she'd been married to the star quarterback of the Jacksonville Jacks, Trey Christopher. Even if she hadn't been married, she was as far out of Niko's league as Lesley Robinson.

But Lesley's here, his subconscious reminded him, *with you.*

"I knew Hayley through her stepsister, Stephanie."

"You and Stephanie dated, then?"

Niko glanced at Lesley briefly. "Why do you assume every woman I mention is someone I dated?"

"I don't know. Isn't it unusual for an unattached, heterosexual man to be just friends with women?"

"Maybe. Probably."

"So?"

"So what?"

"You and Stephanie dated?"

Niko realized he should have thought up an explanation to cover Lesley's inquiries before now. What could he tell her? That he'd never dated Stephanie, but he'd loved her? That he'd done his best to protect her from Carlos Mariano even though she was Carlos' woman? He didn't know how to explain how close he'd been to Stephanie, close enough to have a child with her. A child who was now being raised by Steffie's sister?

Would Lesley understand how Steffie's death from a heroin overdose affected him? He'd never been able to claim Fletcher as his child. Testifying against Carlos guaranteed Fletcher would have a future. Niko's relationship with Steffie changed the course of his life, but he'd never actually dated her.

"It's kind of complicated," he said, hoping to offset Lesley's curiosity. "I'll tell you about it sometime."

"I'd like that."

No, you won't. It's a grim, ugly story from my past, and it will probably send you running.

Maybe that's why he'd shied away from anything

serious with a woman since he'd left Jacksonville. He didn't want to share things better left in the past. But women always wanted to know everything about a guy's history.

If he told the ice-cream-cool and perfect Lesley his sordid story, it would tarnish her somehow. She'd probably never seen or heard anything like it in her life.

There was a reason women like her were out of his league. He didn't want to bring her down to his level. Yet he couldn't deny his attraction to her. For the rest of the drive, he second-guessed his decision to invite her and Ricky along today.

But once they arrived at the Braddock's place, Niko was glad he'd invited Lesley and Ricky because everyone else in Hayley's gathering was either part of a couple or a child. Her brother-in-law Rick and his wife Kaylee were there, their daughter Molly and four-year-old son Tyler. Haylee introduced them to her in-laws, Cal and Lena. Hayley remained close to her ex-in-laws Andy and Lynn as well, which explained why their son, her ex-husband Trey was there along with his wife Baylee. It was one big, happy family gathering, and Niko wondered how they pulled it off.

They'd rented condos in an enclave with a swimming pool surrounded by umbrella tables and chairs along with a barbecue grill. The younger children were supervised by twelve-year-old Molly, who shuttled them from the pool to the beach and back, never venturing far from the adults.

Ricky and Fletcher teamed up immediately, trying to outdo each other skim boarding. Lesley wowed Niko when she changed into a shimmering aquamarine one-piece that complemented her skin tone and figure.

As lunchtime approached, the women gathered at one of the umbrella tables with cold drinks while the men convened near the barbecue grill. Ray tended racks of ribs for the adults and hot dogs for the kids.

Niko nursed a can of soda from a cooler filled with them and chose a position where he could see both the beach and the pool. He watched Fletcher while keeping track of the men's conversation and pretending to be part of the group. A few times he glanced Lesley's way to find her gaze on him. Each time she smiled or inclined her head at him or gave him a little wave, which he acknowledged.

Conversation flowed around him when they sat down to eat. Niko found he didn't have to contribute much. He was an outsider here, not related to anyone. Except Fletcher. The kids gathered at a table of their own, the two boys laughing and cutting up. He'd never seen Ricky as relaxed as he was in Fletcher's company.

He smiled at their antics before he tore his gaze from them, only to have it clash with Lesley's. She smiled at him as if she understood before turning her attention back to her meal.

Everyone helped clean up and carry leftovers to the kitchen. Niko lingered, hoping to have a private word with Hayley. The opportunity presented itself when she offered to show him the view from the second-floor deck. He followed her up the stairs and through a set of French doors overlooking the beach. The warm wind blew stronger at this height, and they saw Fletcher and Ricky once again on the skim boards.

"He's doing fine," Hayley said as they leaned against the railing, watching the boys.

"I can see that."

"Hey, Dad, watch this," Fletcher called. Below them Ray appeared on the beach along with his brother. Fletcher ran toward his skim board, splashing through the water along the shore, stepping on it and skimming along for several feet before it skidded to a halt.

"Impressive," Ray called to him. "You're getting pretty good."

Fletcher grinned and retrieved his board to set up for another round.

"Ray adores him," Hayley said.

"Looks like it's mutual."

"You should be proud."

"Of what?" Niko asked. "I didn't do anything."

Hayley slanted a look up at him from behind her sunglasses. "You persuaded Carlos to let him go. You made sure Carlos couldn't hurt him."

"I didn't have a choice."

"I know you think you didn't. But not every man would have made the choices you did."

"You were the best choice for him. You and Ray."

"That doesn't mean it was easy for you."

Niko continued to watch the boys on the beach. Hayley's compassion made it hard for him to speak. She must have sensed that because she went on. "I see glimpses of you in him. The same kind of protective instincts. His sense of right and wrong. I never have to wonder if Fletcher will do what's right."

That was good to know, Niko decided, refusing to allow the lump in his throat to get the better of him.

"When he's older..." Hayley hesitated a moment before she went on. "I want him to know who you are. Would that be all right with you?"

He managed to get "okay" out without losing it.

He felt her gaze on him before it moved past him to follow his.

Rick and Ray started a game of Frisbee and the two boys joined them. Ricky was horrible at it, but no one seemed to mind. He happily ran after the neon-green disc each time he missed a catch.

After a few minutes, Niko straightened away from the railing and faced Hayley. "Thank you for inviting us today. I'm glad I got to see him, see how he's doing."

Hayley squeezed his hand. "I am, too."

****

When they got back outside, Lesley suggested a short stroll on the beach before they left. Once they were out of earshot of the others, she said, "He's yours, isn't he? Fletcher?"

Niko kept walking, realizing he didn't give Lesley enough credit. She didn't miss anything. "Biologically, yes," he said quietly. "How did you know?"

"You were so interested in him, the way you watched him. At first I thought it was Ricky you were keeping an eye on, but then I realized it was Fletcher. So I started watching him too, and it clicked."

"You're too smart for your own good. Too observant, too."

"I learned to be," Lesley said cryptically. They walked in silence for a little way before she said, "Plus, there's a physical resemblance. He's got your smile, for one thing."

"Does he?"

"And there's something about the way he carries himself. Full of confidence."

Niko laughed.

"Plus he's got this cocky glint in his eye. Just like

184

you."

"Now you're making stuff up," Niko insisted.

"Oh, no." Lesley glanced up at him, her expression full of amusement. "There's definitely a glint."

****

On the way home, Ricky fell asleep in the back seat before they reached the interstate. Lesley lowered the radio volume so it was mere background noise and angled herself toward Niko. "That's why you want to start the community center, why it's so important to you, isn't it? Because of Fletcher."

"There are a lot of reasons."

"But not getting to raise your own son…that has to be one of them," Lesley said almost as if she was speaking to herself. Louder she said, "Does Fletcher know? About you?"

"I don't think so, but he will someday, when he's older. He knows he's adopted. He knows his mother died. Steffie was Hayley's stepsister. Hayley took custody of Fletcher after she died. She didn't think she was up to the challenge of raising someone else's child either." His gaze flickered to Lesley's.

"What changed her mind?"

"You'd have to ask her."

Lesley turned in her seat to check on Ricky. From the rearview mirror, Niko saw Ricky was out like a light, his hair mussed, his cheeks slightly sunburned even though Lesley had coated him with sunscreen.

"Maybe she loved him. Maybe that's why she decided to keep him."

His gaze flickered to her again. "That's as good a reason as any, isn't it?"

"Yes," she said. "I think it is."

Chapter Nineteen

Ricky was asleep and the house had settled for the night when Lesley tapped on Mitzi's bedroom door. "Mother, I need to talk to you."

"Of course, darling. Come in."

Lesley entered and closed the door gently behind her. Her mother was propped up in bed with several pillows behind her, the lamp on the nightstand giving off a warm glow. Scattered across the covers were several catalogs, fashion magazines, and a mystery novel open and lying face down. The television, set into a wall unit comprised of shelves and cabinets, was tuned to a twenty-four-hour news channel, the volume set on low, completely ignored by Mitzi.

As if she hadn't surrounded herself with enough distractions, her mother held an emery board in one hand and frowned at the glossy polish on her index finger.

Lesley pulled a small upholstered chair closer to the bed. She slid her palms against her thighs, covered now in pajama bottoms.

"A pajama party, darling?" Mitzi asked, taking in Lesley's attire. "Are we going to share secrets and gossip? Tell me about your trip to Sarasota. Did you have fun? I wouldn't mind hearing about what goes on those nights you sneak out to meet that divine young man of yours, either."

"What? I don't—"

"Why, of course you do. Who could blame you? Certainly not me." Mitzi reached across and patted her hand. "Don't worry, darling. Your secret's safe."

Lesley stared at her lap. Her cheeks flamed in embarrassment. She'd thought she was being so clever, so sly. If Mitzi knew she'd been sneaking out to meet with Niko, then so did Lita. So, surely, did Mitch. Everyone knew.

She'd put off talking to her mother, but Niko's words earlier bolstered her courage. Or so she'd thought.

"Darling, what is it? What's wrong? Did Niko—"

"This isn't about Niko. God!" Lesley buried her face in her hands. Why did her mother always manage to turn the tables on her?

"Sweetheart, I didn't mean to…"

"Didn't mean to what?" Lesley snapped. "Embarrass me? Bring up a subject I'd obviously taken pains to keep to myself?"

Mitzi closed her eyes and sighed. "I don't…"

At that moment, she noticed how tired her mother looked. How old. Without her makeup and jewelry, her designer clothes and handbags. A wave of sympathy shot through her. Mitzi might not have been the kind of mother Lesley longed for, but she hadn't been the kind of daughter Mitzi probably wanted either. Mitzi would have loved a daughter who would curl up in bed with her and share secrets and gossip. Lesley had been too busy being her father's daughter, being smart and successful and honing her business savvy. She'd never wanted to be a social butterfly, never been interested in shopping or lunching with the girls.

Barbara Meyers

But her mother was just as successful socially as Lesley was in business. Perhaps they should have set their differences aside and embraced each other in spite of them. Niko was right. Mitzi was a survivor, navigating her way through Richard's illness and managing to create a life for herself without him. Lesley was smacked with the revelation that she didn't know what she'd have done these past few years without her mother to anchor everything.

"Mom, I'm sorry."

Mitzi opened her eyes and smiled sadly. "You never call me Mom. Not since you were a know-it-all teenager rolling your eyes at my antiquated ways and ridiculous questions."

"I'm a lousy daughter." *A lousy mother. A lousy girlfriend.*

"No, darling. Not at all. You're just—you. And I'm me. We're very different, that's all."

"But the same in some ways."

"I suppose." After a moment Mitzi said, "Anyway, what did you want to talk about?"

Lesley removed the picture from the pocket of her robe. "Have you ever seen this before?"

Mitzi took the paper and gazed at it for a moment squinting before she reluctantly picked up a pair of reading glasses to examine it more closely. "Yes. Yes, I have. Where did you get this?"

"From Maria."

"Maria?"

"Yes. The day she showed up here and wanted to see Daddy. She practically threw it in my face when she left."

"You've had it all this time?"

"I wasn't sure it meant anything until now." Lesley looked away from her mother's gaze.

"But now?"

"I think the woman in the picture is Maria's mother. Recently I found out that Daddy set up a bank account years ago. Monthly transfers were made to a bank in San Salvador."

Mitzi frowned. "Are you sure about that?"

"Yes."

"You think there's a connection? Between your father and Maria's mother?"

"Of course I do! Don't you?"

"What exactly is it you want to know?"

"Mother!" Lesley shoved her fingers into her hair and tugged at it in frustration. Mitzi could be so obtuse at times. "Is Daddy Maria's father?"

"Of course not!" Mitzi looked appalled.

Lesley wasn't entirely convinced. "You're sure?"

Mitzi sighed as if she shouldn't have to explain. "Your father and I don't keep secrets from one another."

"Ever? You're saying Daddy tells you everything and you do the same with him."

"Well…" Mitzi looked a little less sure of herself. "There might have been a few things over the years I specifically told him I didn't want to know about."

"Maria's mother being one of those things."

"In a way. But darling, you don't have the whole picture."

Mitzi pushed back the covers and got out of bed, pulling her negligee over her matching nightgown. She went to the row of cabinets at the bottom of the entertainment shelves and began opening them. Photo albums were stacked one on top of another in each cabinet. She pulled two from the third cabinet and set them at the foot of the bed.

"I think it's either in this one…" She flipped through the pages, the plastic covering, old and brittle, making a sticky noise as they moved. "Must be this one." She opened the other album and searched the pages. "Here." She put her finger on one and handed the album to Lesley.

She stared at the yellowed newspaper clipping beneath the photo. It was the same photograph. Her father. Maria's mother. And another man with his arm around Maria's mother. There was a headline above the photo. "Robinson Group Expands Operations to Central America." The article was from the *Pittsburgh Times*, where the Robinson Group was headquartered. Lesley stared at the other man in the picture. "That's Uncle Brad."

"Yes." Mitzi put the other photo album away and climbed back into bed.

"Is he—was he—Maria's father?"

Lesley handed the album back to her. Mitzi gazed lovingly at the picture of her husband and drew a finger along his image. "Your father was so excited about opening the textile plant there. He and Brad made several trips down there once they'd settled on the location in San Salvador. Maria's mother Elena was hired as a foreman. I met her once. Briefly. Pretty, vivacious, smart. Brad was smitten. For a while anyway. Even though your father warned him repeatedly not to swim in the company pool, well, that was Brad.

"Richard always wanted to think the best of his

little brother. Give him a chance to show what he could do. He gave him chance after chance after chance, and Brad blew them all."

"I remember the last time Uncle Brad visited us. He and Daddy were in the den, and I heard them shouting through the closed door."

Mitzi nodded. "Before the accident. Your father let him oversee the operation in San Salvador against his better judgment. Brad insisted he could handle it, would handle it.

"Brad was the baby of the family. He had no self-discipline. No real moral code. Oh, but he was a charmer, especially with women. You can imagine the women hired to work in the plant were easy pickings for a man like him."

"I adored Uncle Brad," Lesley admitted. "He made me feel special. Told me I was pretty. He'd tickle me or touch my hair and I'd be giddy."

"You were only four. Imagine being fourteen or twenty-four and having this devastatingly attractive man tell you everything you want to hear. That you're pretty and desirable. Brad went through a lot of women. Broke a lot of hearts."

"Including Maria's mother's, apparently."

"Yes. That shouting match you remember? She'd informed Richard that she was pregnant with Brad's child. She expected Brad to marry her, probably because he'd led her to believe he would, but he had no intention of being tied down to some 'peasant woman,' as I believe he referred to her.

"Richard told him this was it. Either he took responsibility for the situation or they were done.

"Brad left angry. The rest you know. He headed

straight for the nearest bar. Drank too much. Wrapped his car around a telephone pole.

"Your uncle was a sore spot between your father and me. I'd told him years before that I didn't want to know about any of his problems with his brother. I was sick of watching your father agonize over and take responsibility for his brother's choices. After Brad died, we never discussed him or what he'd done. Your father was torn up about it and racked with guilt for something I believe to this day he thought he could prevent."

"So Daddy…"

"Based on what you've told me, I have a feeling he tried to make things right with Elena. He kept her on at the plant. Set up that account to compensate her for what Brad did. In return he probably asked her to keep the truth about Brad secret, and I would imagine that she agreed."

"Daddy must have brought Maria here," Lesley said, trying to piece together the sequence of events.

"I wouldn't be surprised. He'd probably have helped her find other work eventually, too, if that's what she wanted."

"Because she was Brad's daughter. And he probably still felt guilty."

"I'm sure."

"So Maria didn't know she was related to us?"

"I can't say if she did or not. I assume Elena kept her end of the deal." Mitzi pointed to the picture Lesley held. "Probably why she ripped Brad out of that picture."

"Then after Elena died, Maria saw the picture of her mother and Daddy and jumped to conclusions."

"Easy enough to do."

"The money in the account ran out. That's why she's here now. That's why she wanted to see Daddy so badly. She thought he'd give her more money. She believes he's her father."

Mitzi grew thoughtful for a moment. "Tomorrow, let's go through your father's private files. I have the keys to his desk, but I never wanted to use them." Her gaze met Lesley's. "Not unless I had to."

Lesley squeezed Mitzi's hand. "I understand, Mom. If Daddy were able, what do you think he'd do?"

Mitzi frowned, closed the album and pushed it away. "Your father was more than generous with Brad. He was more than generous with Maria's mother. And frankly, with Maria herself. It's possible Maria has a lot of Brad in her. She's proven she's impulsive and without self-discipline. Nor does she want to take responsibility for her mistakes."

"She's still his niece," Lesley said.

"Your cousin. Ricky's biological mother. She's family, that's true. Your father might help her some more, but he learned his lesson with Brad. Sometimes when you help people too much, it's to their detriment. We all have to make our own lives, our own choices, and live with the consequences."

Chapter Twenty

Mitch tapped on Lesley's office door, which was slightly ajar. She was almost finished with a conference call and motioned him in. He took a seat across from her. As he rarely sought her out in the middle of the afternoon, it must be of some importance.

The moment the call concluded, she looked at him expectantly. "Everything all right?"

"I'm not sure," he said. "When I arrived at the school to pick up Ricky, a woman was talking to him. It was Maria Delgado."

Shocked, Lesley asked, "How could she be at the school? How could she get that close to him? Mitch, how certain are you it was her?"

"I was about ninety-five percent sure before I asked Ricky about it. He confirmed it was the same woman who talked to him in the park that day. The one Niko confronted at the pier."

"Any idea what she was doing at his school?"

"Not really. Ricky said she asked him how he liked going to school there, about his teachers, that sort of thing."

"I'm calling Susan Walters, right now. I'll get to the bottom of this."

Lesley found the principal's number in her directory and auto-dialed. She put the call on speaker.

She was connected almost immediately. "Lesley,

how can I help you?"

"Susan. Thank you for taking my call. There was an incident during pickup this afternoon that has me concerned, and I wanted to ask you about it. I have my chief of security, Mitch Hayes, here with me."

"All right. I'll help however I can, but I haven't had any reports of any incidents this afternoon."

"It concerns a woman named Maria Delgado."

"I recognize the name. I had an appointment with her earlier."

"May I ask in regard to what?"

"Forgive me, Lesley, but what is this about?"

"Did you tell her she could speak to the children?"

"I didn't tell her she couldn't."

Lesley knew she needed to tread carefully. "Mitch was concerned because he saw Maria—that is, Ms. Delgado speaking with Ricky. We've had a few incidents in the past where Ricky has been approached by strangers who engage him in conversation, try to earn his trust, that sort of thing." Lesley made a helpless gesture at Mitch. She was winging it, and they both knew it.

"Of course. I'm sure Ms. Delgado had no ulterior motives. Most likely Ricky was simply approachable. She's relocating to the area, and she has a son in first grade."

"Oh?"

"I gave her a brief tour. Nothing unusual, really. She made it clear it was important to her to find a school that would be the best fit for her son."

"I see." Were there no lengths to which Maria would not go to achieve her goal?

"Lesley, is there something you're not telling me

about this woman? Is there an issue with our security arrangements? Because we take the safety of our students very seriously."

"Of course you do." Susan obviously sensed Lesley was holding back, but she didn't feel obligated to share any further details. "As I said, there have been a few minor incidents with Ricky in the past, nothing to do with the school, mind you. I simply feel I can't be too careful."

"I understand. Is there anything else I can help you with?" Susan asked.

"No. You've told me what I needed to know. Thank you for your help."

After Lesley hung up, Mitch looked as grim as Lesley felt. "This makes me nervous," she said. "What is Maria up to?"

"I'd say she wants us, that is you, to know how easy it is for her to get close to Ricky. First it was the park. Then the pier. Now at his school. She's sending you a message."

"For what purpose, though? She surely has no intention of kidnapping him. She knows she'd be our first suspect."

"I think it might be a good idea to ask her."

"How do we find her?"

"Willow Bay isn't that big. If she's here on a temporary visa, she's probably found seasonal work. If I was still with the sheriff's office, I could locate her fairly easily."

"You're saying Niko could."

"He would be faster, certainly."

"I'll ask him."

"I wouldn't mind paying her a visit, if you want.

I'd like to know what it is she's after."

"Let me talk to Niko and get back to you."

****

That night when Lesley went in to say goodnight to Ricky, he looked up from his book and tracked her intently. She sat on the edge of his bed and smoothed his hair back. His gaze never left hers. "Everything okay?" she asked.

"Do you know who my father is?"

Lesley tried to hide her surprise. "Why do you ask?"

"That lady? The one who talked to me at the park? When she was at my school today, she said she knew who my daddy was."

The wave of hatred for Maria that swept through Lesley shocked her. She wanted to hurt Maria. Badly. She envisioned wrapping her fingers around her neck. Lesley never cared much about Maria's reckless behavior in the past, but now she was able to hurt Ricky. Every protective instinct Lesley had rose up in defense of him. She'd always expected to explain the circumstances of his birth at some point in the future because she knew he'd have questions. She'd never planned to lie to him. But he was only six. How was she supposed to explain in terms he could understand?

"I do know who he is," she began. Ricky laid his book aside and settled back on his pillows as if readying himself for a bedtime story. "I was going to explain this to you when you were older."

"I know you're not my mom," Ricky said. He must have seen something in Lesley's expression because he hastened to add, "I mean, you are my mom. But you didn't…"

197

"It's okay. I know what you mean. I won't lie to you, Ricky, ever. How about that? How about if we make a promise to each other right now to never lie to each other?"

Ricky nodded vigorously.

"Sometimes the truth is hard. Sometimes it's hurtful. But in the end, it's still the best thing to tell the truth."

He went back to watching her closely, as if he suspected she was trying to distract him from his original question.

"Your father," she said, lifting an eyebrow in question, making sure he still wanted to know. When he nodded, she continued, "Is a man I used to be married to. His name is Steven."

Ricky frowned, his disappointment obvious. "Oh."

"Do you want me to go on?"

"I guess."

"What's wrong?"

"I thought…maybe…"

"Go on."

"I thought maybe it was Niko."

Stunned, Lesley listened as Ricky rushed on. "I thought that's why he showed up all of a sudden. Why he does stuff with me, like he liked me. I thought maybe…" Ricky looked away.

"What?"

"I thought he didn't know before."

"Oh, sweetheart." Lesley knew she was ill-equipped for dealing with this situation, for having this conversation, but she was determined to make it through.

"I can understand why you'd wish Niko was your

dad." *I wish he was, too.* What a different life Ricky would have if Niko had fathered him, been a father to him. She thought about that for a moment, wondering if her assessment was true. Six years ago? Where had Niko been? What had he been doing? Maybe he wouldn't have been in a position to take on responsibility for Ricky. The only thing Lesley knew for sure was that Niko would have wanted to.

"Honey, we don't have to talk about this right now if you don't want to."

"You said you'd tell me."

"I know. I thought you might have decided you didn't want to know right now."

"No. I still do."

"Okay, then." Lesley paused for a moment, praying she'd say the words right, that she wouldn't scar Ricky for life with her blundering recitation of the facts. "That lady? Her name is Maria. She used to work here. She was Lita's helper before you were born. Back before Grandpa got sick. She and my husband, um, liked each other. They, um, made a baby together."

"Me?"

Lesley smiled and squeezed his hand. "You." He didn't let go. "Then a whole bunch of stuff happened. You were sick when you were born. Maria came here from another country, and she couldn't stay to take care of you. She asked me to, and I said I would. Then Grandpa got sick, too, and I had to run the company." Lesley ran out of steam. She didn't know where to go with the story.

Ricky processed what she'd told him, then asked, "Where's Steven? Why didn't he take care of me?"

"He didn't want to," Lesley said simply. There was

no way she could think of to soften the truth.

"Did you?"

"Not at first. That's the truth. I didn't even know about you until you were here. It was hard for me, Ricky. Lita and Missy took care of you most of the time when you were little. I know they still do. But I'm glad you're here with us. With me. I'm glad you're my son. Someday, I hope you can be glad I'm your mother."

"I am." They hugged for a long time.

"I love you, Ricky," she whispered against his hair.

"I love you too, Mom."

She let him go. "Get some sleep, okay? And remember, you and me." She pointed back and forth between them. "We always tell each other the truth."

He smiled. "Okay."

****

Niko watched from the shadows as several employees of the Willow Bay Beach Club Hotel exited the service entrance in a cluster. They called out farewells in Spanish before dispersing into the parking lot. Two of them stuck together, sharing a ride. The other three split up, heading for their vehicles.

Maria had parked her older model compact near one of the security floodlights. A smart move on her part, but her car wasn't near any of her coworkers' vehicles. They'd be headed out of the parking lot before she unlocked her door.

He didn't want to frighten, threaten, or intimidate the woman, only wanted to talk to her. He wanted to know what she wanted and what it would take for her to leave the Robinson family alone. For good.

Her keys were at the ready as she walked with confidence to the driver's side of her car. Niko stepped forward from behind the minivan in the next space. Maria gasped and backed up a step, fumbling in her big purse for something. A can of pepper spray, he figured.

Using a low tone, he spoke to her in Spanish. "I'm not here to hurt you. I only want to talk."

"You. You're that cop." She tossed her head and sneered. "Still sniffing around Miss Lesley?" She gave him a look of disdain. Even in her work uniform, an unimpressive green polo shirt with the hotel's logo on the sleeve and white slacks, Maria Delgado managed to project the image that she didn't belong here doing menial labor. She was better than everyone around her. They just hadn't realized it yet. Bull-headed arrogance draped itself around her and dripped off. Niko flexed his fingers. Five seconds in her presence and he wanted nothing more than to wipe that smug expression off her face.

"Maybe I can help you."

"I do not need your help."

"What is it you want, Maria?"

"That is not your business. I do not have to talk to you."

"No. Of course you don't."

He advanced a few steps, and Maria retreated. He was close to blocking the driver's door. Her gaze flickered uncertainly over him and then to the door of her car. He hadn't convinced her he wouldn't hurt her if she tried to get past him. But she hadn't withdrawn any pepper spray either.

"What's your plan? Going to keep showing up, trying to make contact with Ricky? Are you planning to kidnap him?"

"No!"

"You think if you keep threatening to take your story to the press, the Robinsons will just roll over and write you a check?"

Her shocked stare told him he'd nailed her.

"You're in over your head, Maria. Whatever you think you know, whatever you think you can get, it won't work. You keep it up, don't be surprised when Lesley has you charged with harassment. First you'll go to jail. Then you'll be deported. Again. They'll pull your work visa, red flag your file, and you'll never be allowed back in the US. Is that what you want?"

Niko wasn't actually certain any of that would happen, but she probably didn't know that. Then again, maybe she'd done her homework better than he had.

Maria held her ground, lifted her chin and stared him down. "I have done nothing wrong." She glanced over her shoulder as a security cart rolled into view to begin an unhurried check up and down each row of vehicles. "I am leaving." She charged toward him, her keys clenched between her fingers and pointed at him. Niko obligingly backed up, raising his hands as he went.

She unlocked the vehicle and got in, throwing a highly descriptive and unflattering epithet about the circumstances of his conception at him.

****

When Lesley got out of the bath later, she discovered a missed call from Niko. She held her cell phone in her hand and stared at the display. She wanted to see him. Badly. She wanted to tell him about her conversation with Ricky. She wanted to know if he'd seen Maria.

She wanted—oh, how she wanted—to walk into

his house and into his arms. To be held and to hold. To talk and to listen and to share. She wanted to lie in bed and listen to the beat of his heart and get turned on all over again just from the touch of his skin against hers.

She fought a nightly battle with herself. Steeling herself not to call him. Warning herself away. Telling herself tonight she wouldn't sneak out of her house and into his bed. She wouldn't drag herself home at some shameful hour and pretend she'd never left. It was embarrassing. She was addicted. She was in love. She was terrified.

She hadn't considered the kind of power she wielded as the head of one of the most successful companies in the country. Beyond her family's personal wealth, she possessed far-reaching influence in many areas, and with that came the ability to affect a large number of lives.

But at the moment she only cared about one, and wondered how a romantic entanglement with her would affect Niko if it ever became public. There would be problems unless it was handled in the exact right way. She'd lain awake for hours, trying to figure out what the exact right way was. She hadn't approached any of her PR people for their input. Yet. But she feared she was inching closer to a time when she'd have to.

Her worse fear was that involvement with her would somehow make a mockery of everything Niko was trying to achieve with the Challenge Project. The press could be brutal if the story spun the wrong way— the gold-digging fundraiser, the slumming business mogul, or something equally unkind. Niko might never find his way out of a storm of bad press. Her reputation and that of her company could easily weather such a storm. It'd be nothing more than a brief shower in the scope of their broad umbrella. But Niko was more or less out there on his own with no such protection. He could drown.

Still, all of the power she wielded in the business world was nothing compared to her feelings for Niko Morales.

Her phone vibrated, signaling an incoming text.

—*You still up?*—

Niko.

Lesley smiled. —*Yes*—

—*Me too*—

Lesley laughed at his statement of the obvious, as he knew she would. It might be the first time she had laughed all day. Why would she deprive herself of that? Why should she? That was something she couldn't answer. Unless the answer was she shouldn't and wouldn't.

While she'd been thinking and Niko had been waiting for her next response, he'd texted

—*???*—

—*I'm coming over*— she typed back.

He replied with a smiling emoji.

****

Niko was waiting for her, and she was in his arms the moment the door closed behind her. She didn't know how Niko knew, except he seemed to be attuned to her in a way no one else was, but he held her tight against him for a long time. Exactly what she wanted. She breathed in his scent, her arms around his neck. Eventually, they broke apart and she gave a little laugh. "Thanks. I needed that."

"Me, too." He led her down the hall. "Want

something to drink?"

"Not really. Unless you do."

"No. Where are we going?"

"Bedroom? But I've got something to tell you."

"I've got something to tell you too."

They lay close together, facing each other. Niko must have installed the lowest wattage bulb he could find in the bedside lamp because it gave off just enough light to allow them to see each other and nothing more. Niko was more in shadows because the light was on his side.

"You first."

"I found Maria. Talked to her."

"Already? When?"

"Tonight. When she got off work."

"What'd she say? Tell me everything."

Niko did, concluding with, "I didn't get much out of her. Probably just pissed her off even more. But at least I know where she lives and works now. It'll be easier to keep an eye on her."

Lesley watched Niko carefully. "Maria told Ricky she knows who his father is."

"That's low even for her. Why would she do something like that?"

"I don't know."

"He asked about it, I assume."

Lesley nodded.

"What'd you tell him?"

"The truth."

"Oh, babe." His eyes were full of sympathy. He ran his fingers through her hair. "That must have been tough."

"I couldn't lie to him. But he's so young. I hope

this doesn't scar him."

"He's tougher than he lets on. He beat the odds when he was born, didn't he? He'll probably keep on doing that. Plus he's your son."

"What does that mean?"

"It means you'll always have his back. That means a lot to a kid."

She stroked his arm. "Speaking as someone who never had it?"

"Exactly."

"Want to hear something funny? Not funny, really. Touching." His expression said yes, so she went on. "Ricky hoped you were his father. He thought that was why you started coming around, spending time with him."

She could see the emotion in Niko's eyes, felt herself falling over a precipice, praying he'd never stop being the safe place for her to land. "Want to know something else? I kept thinking how lucky he'd have been if you were."

They moved together then, tenderly. No one was in a hurry tonight.

Chapter Twenty-One

"Thank you for meeting me," Lesley said as she slid into the booth across from Steven. "I wasn't exactly gracious the last time."

"You had your reasons," he replied.

"I assume you're still in contact with Maria."

"Not if I can help it. But I haven't been able to get rid of her either."

A server approached, and Lesley ordered sparkling water with lime again. While she waited for her drink, she took a good look at her ex-husband. "Are you all right?"

"Yes. Why?"

"You look a bit pale."

"I'm fine."

Her drink appeared, and when the server determined they needed nothing else, she left. Lesley took the photocopy of the picture Mitzi had found out of her purse and slid it across to Steven. He stared at it for a moment before looking up. "What's this?"

"It's a copy of the original picture. The one Maria had was torn before it was copied. As you can see, there's another man in the picture."

"With his arm around Maria's mother," Steven commented.

"It's my father's younger brother. His name was Bradley."

"Why do I think there's more you want to tell me?"

"Bradley was involved with Maria's mother. She was a foreman at the textile plant the Robinson Group operated in El Salvador. Uncle Brad admitted to my father Maria's mother was pregnant by him. They fought about it. Brad died shortly afterward."

"But Maria was certain your father sent money to her mother."

"He did. He felt responsible. Since Bradley wasn't alive to do the right thing, my father stepped in and made sure Maria's mother had enough money to support herself and her daughter. He helped bring Maria here to work, but he had an agreement with her mother. Maria was not to know she was related to us. Apparently her mother kept her promise."

Steven glanced at the picture again. "Until she died anyway. Maria found this picture and assumed your father was her father."

"I believe so, yes. My father funded an account several years ago. I only learned of it a few days ago when the bank called because the money ran out."

"Maria figured there was more where that came from."

Lesley sipped her drink overwhelmed with relief. She'd hated thinking Maria had been wronged by her family, by her own father. But she'd also been given advantages by Richard, and she'd made some bad decisions. Including her involvement with Steven.

She chose her words carefully. "If you see Maria, I'd like you to relay what I've just shared. You can take the copy of the picture and give it to her. I'd like you to also relay that we do not feel she's owed anything more from us. Not the Robinson family or the company. If she continues to make threats and allegations, if she goes to the press with her accusations, I will bring the full brunt of our legal department down on her, and it won't be pretty."

"She already went to the press."

"She did? When?"

"I'm not sure exactly. Last week a *Tribune* reporter cornered me. Told me he had an email conversation with someone claiming to have a story involving me and you. Asked if he'd be interested. He kept it vague, hoping I'd give something away, no doubt."

"And?"

"That was it. I played it off like there'd always be detractors trying to ruin my chance at a Senate run. And for someone in your position, it comes with the territory. Good news is I don't think he had enough to run with a story yet."

"But if he follows up, if he meets with Maria and she tells him everything—"

"We're screwed."

"I won't let her get away with it. She's already caused enough trouble for me."

A smile played at the corners of Steven's mouth. "No, I'm sure you won't." After a moment he said, "There's something different about you, Les. Something that wasn't there when we were together."

"Oh, really?"

"There's a spark, a passion, a light in your eyes. Something."

"Hmm. Yes. Well, be that as it may, could you also tell Maria that I'm open to allowing her to visit Ricky if she'd like. Under supervision, of course."

"Why?"

"Why? Because she forced my hand when she told Ricky she knew who his biological father is."

"What?" Steven went from pale to ashen. He'd never had a weak stomach, but he looked like he might need to dash to the men's room.

"Yes. She showed up at Ricky's school for a guided tour. She spoke to him while he was waiting in the pickup line."

"Ah, hell."

"I told him the truth."

Steven squirmed and swallowed visibly.

Lesley went on. "If she's interested, I'll see what I can do. Ricky may not want to have anything to do with her, of course, and I'd abide by his wishes."

"What about me?"

"What about you?"

"Are you going to make the same offer to me?"

"I didn't think you were interested in meeting him."

"I'm not. I just wondered, if I was, whether you'd allow it."

Lesley leaned across the table. "Look, Steven, I won't lie to him. He'd never asked about his biological parents before, but now he knows you're his biological father and that you wanted nothing to do with him. Thank Maria for that."

"That's great. Someday he'll be able to ruin me, too."

"Ruin you? What are you talking about?"

"Nothing. But that one indiscretion is going to follow me around for the rest of my life."

Lesley stared at him dumbfounded. Just when she'd thought maybe there was a shred of decency in her former husband, that maybe he wasn't the completely self-centered ass he'd shown himself to be time and again, he proved her wrong. She fumbled for her wallet.

"Yes, Steven," she spat as she threw several dollars on the table to pay for her drink, "it's all about you. It's always been about you. You never think about how your one indiscretion affected more lives than just yours." She stood and stared at him. "I'm just so glad you are out of my life."

She strode out the door, vibrating with fury. Her heart bled for Ricky for having been born to two overwhelmingly selfish and self-serving individuals such as Maria and Steven. They hadn't wanted him and didn't deserve him. She hadn't wanted him either, at first, but that had changed. She vowed to give him everything they couldn't and wouldn't. She sincerely hoped, given the opportunity, Ricky would turn his back on meeting either one of them, the same way they'd turned their backs on him.

She was feeling wild and reckless. When she got to her car, she punched in Niko's number. She glanced at her watch. He should be home by now. He answered on the third ring. She got right to it. "I'd like you to come for dinner if you're free tonight."

"Where?"

"At my house."

Niko hesitated. "Are you sure? I mean, do you think that's a good idea?"

"I think it's a splendid idea. I'm going to see if my mother can be there. And Mitch. Ricky, of course."

Again Niko hesitated. "Are you feeling all right? What's going on?"

Lesley sighed. "Niko, I—" Now it was her turn to hesitate. She couldn't put what she felt into words, except that she'd set herself on a road to change her life the moment she'd met Niko Morales. She was afraid of it, but she wanted to embrace it at the same time. She hated hiding and pretending and not getting what she wanted and not being who she was. "I can't really explain it," she told him. "Except Ricky adores you. We all do," she rushed on. "I'd like to have something like a family dinner with all the people I care about together."

Lesley waited through a long pause. She could almost hear Niko absorbing her words, trying to analyze them. But he didn't question her further. He simply said, "What time?"

Next she called Lita and told her the plan. They agreed on a menu, and Lesley stopped at the market on her way home. It took her much longer to shop since she wasn't familiar with the store layout, but she found what she needed and headed home.

Lita helped her unload everything. Her mother and Mitch were both available to join them. "I'll change and come and help you," Lesley told Lita.

The other woman smiled. "Miss Lesley, no offense, but you not be much help. You go play with Ricky, or maybe I let you set the table or something. I cook."

Lesley hugged Lita's shoulders. "You know me too well. All right then, I'll be back in a little while."

In her room she shed her suit, her jewelry, and her high heels. She donned a linen sundress and sandals. In the bathroom, she touched up her makeup, unclipped her hair and ran a brush through it. She reached for the clip but didn't pick it up. She'd leave her hair down tonight.

She found Ricky in his room, playing an educational computer game. She came and sat on the bed beside him. He stared at her.

"What?" she asked.

"You look pretty."

"Thank you. I invited Niko to dinner," she told him. "Mitch and Grandma will be there, too. Lita's making pasta."

"The kind I like?"

"Angel hair with shrimp, yes."

"Why's Niko coming?"

"Because I like him. And you like him."

"And he likes us."

"Yes."

"You never invited him before."

"No. But I invited him now, and he said he'd come. There's a first time for everything."

Ricky indicated the computer game. "Want to play?"

"Sure. But you'll have to show me how." She sidled up next to Ricky and put her arm around him.

****

They were an odd group, Lesley decided. She looked at them all gathered around the table. Her mother and Mitch. Her and Niko. Lita and Ricky. Lita initially demurred when Lesley insisted she join them. "You're part of the family. Come and have dinner with us."

They'd laughed and talked and chatted. Mitch and Mitzi had no problem keeping the conversation rolling. Mitzi was at her animated best, clearly enjoying being

213

in the company of two handsome men. Ricky beamed at everyone. Lesley allowed him to slurp strands of angel hair, although she made it clear it was a one-time-only allowance and that doing so was considered very bad manners.

When they'd eaten their fill, Mitzi invited Mitch to watch a movie with her in the media room, and he accepted. Lita took Ricky off to give him a bath. "Want to walk down the beach?" Lesley asked Niko.

"Okay."

They started walking. The light from the setting sun was fading fast. "You were kind of quiet at dinner," she ventured. "Is everything okay?"

"Sure."

She sensed a distance between them that hadn't been there before. Just when Lesley decided she wanted to get close to Niko for real, he retreated. Inviting him to dinner took their relationship to the next level, acknowledging it, at least to her inner circle, bringing it out of hiding. She thought that was what Niko wanted. But maybe she'd been wrong. They strolled farther in a silence she didn't know how to break. They arrived at the pass and turned to head back. "What are you thinking?" she asked. That seemed as safe a question as any.

"I'm thinking I don't fit into your life."

Lesley came to a halt.

"What do you want from me, Lesley? Do you even know? You keep me under wraps for months, but you dress me up and take me out when you need an escort to one your fancy balls. You can show up at my place in the middle of the night and sleep with me, but God forbid anyone should find out about us. You tell me your troubles and you act like you want my help, but at the same time…ah hell." Niko shoved a hand through his hair and started back to the house.

"But at the same time, what?" Lesley caught up with him. She wrapped her fingers around his bicep in an effort to slow him down. Her grip was no match for the solid muscle it met, but Niko stopped anyway.

He stared at her in the murky light before he finally said, "But at the same time, this." He kissed her hard. She thought she could feel every muscle and sinew in his body as he wrapped her tightly against him. Abruptly he pulled away. "I am so fucking in love with you, but as you've pointed out numerous times, we are worlds apart. So how are we going to make this work, huh? You can't tell me because you don't know. Because you don't think it can work. You know where that leaves me? Out in the fucking cold. Without you."

He let her go and took long, determined strides to get back to the house and away from her. She didn't follow him or call after him. She didn't know what to say. Niko rarely swore in her presence, but he'd done it twice just now. He was frustrated and angry, and she couldn't blame him. She wanted to feel warmed all over because he'd said he was in love with her, but the way he said it gave her chills. He wanted a place in her life, but he didn't think there was one. Not unless she created it.

Chapter Twenty-Two

Steven had been about ready to call it a night. He'd
sacked out in front of the television, halfheartedly
reading through case files and doing paperwork. He'd
made no other plans for this Saturday night. His
workload was ridiculous, not that there'd been any
increase in pay or additional staffing.

When he heard a knock, he knew who it was.
Maria stopping by on her way home from work. She'd
gotten on in the housekeeping department at the Willow
Bay Beach Club for the season, working the four-to-
midnight shift.

Steven opened the door and stepped back, sincerely
hoping this would be the last time Maria Delgado
would cross his threshold. She sashayed past, and he
admired her bravado, almost as much as he admired the
swing of her hips. He tamped down the wave of lust she
inspired in him. He refused to give in to the urge he had
every time she showed up: to take her up against the
wall, use that lush body of hers. He liked to believe
he'd learned some self-control these past few years.
Maria Delgado could ruin him.

Perhaps that's what she had in mind. He took a
couple of careful steps toward her. She watched him, no
doubt trying to gauge his mood. He hoped he
successfully hid his thoughts from her. She gave him a
little smile as she stood there in her simple dress and

her strappy sandals.

"I am very lonely since I am here," she said, keeping her gaze on his.

"I'm sorry to hear that. Look, I've got something to tell you," Steven began.

He stopped and stared when she did something he didn't expect. With one motion she tugged the elastic neckline of the dress down to her waist, where it joined the elastic there, and she pushed the entire thing to the floor.

His mouth went dry as she stepped away from the puddle of cloth. "I think you are lonely too," she said softly.

"Maria, don't." He nearly choked on the words.

"Is it so bad?" she asked, "if we make each other not lonely?"

"Maria…"

Her hand closed over his crotch to caress his straining cock. He groaned. Her breasts were barely contained in a lacy black bra. He'd already caught a glimpse of the matching panties.

"Please," she whispered. "I never forget you."

She drew the zipper of his slacks down and slid her hand inside his briefs. She knew exactly what to do because he'd taught her how to please him. On her knees now, she unbuttoned his slacks and they dropped to the floor. She drew his briefs down and looked up at him before she took him in her mouth.

"Oh, God."

He buried his fingers in her hair and let her pleasure him until he couldn't stand it anymore and he pulled back. He didn't even have to tell her. She lay back on the floor and removed her panties, tossing them in the direction of her dress. She lifted her knees and spread her legs. Steven drove into her. He didn't kiss her. Didn't fondle her breasts or suckle her nipples. Didn't even remove her bra. He only wanted this, a quick, hard fuck on an unforgiving surface, to use her body to find his own pleasure, and then he wanted her to go away.

When it was over, when he was spent, he rolled away from her and silently cursed himself. He cursed her as well, wondering what her game was. She knew her power over him. Steven hadn't liked it when it was Lesley, and he didn't like it when it was someone like Maria. Especially since Maria had nothing to offer him except her body. No money. No influence. No powerful friends to fund his campaign. He'd be a senator by now if Maria hadn't ruined it all for him. If she hadn't seduced him, hadn't gotten pregnant. If she hadn't been the reason Lesley kicked him out of her house, her life and access to her fortune.

He had to get rid of Maria somehow. Perhaps in this instance the truth would set him free.

He got up and barely looked at her sprawled there on his living room rug. "Get dressed and come into the kitchen. I've got something to show you."

He pulled his briefs up and put his pants back on, zipping them on the way to the kitchen. He filled a highball glass with ice and poured a couple fingers of bourbon over it. He took a healthy swallow before he heard Maria's high heels on the tile.

She stopped on the other side of the counter and looked at him. He couldn't decipher her expression. Was she disappointed in his lovemaking? Had she expected hearts and flowers? A bed? He didn't know and didn't care.

He pushed the picture Lesley had given him across the counter. "Read it and weep."

She picked it up and studied it before she looked at him again. "What is this?"

"It's what we in the legal business like to call the complete picture, Maria. Something you should have before you start spouting off about who your father is and what you're owed."

Maria's brows knit together. "I do not understand. Who is this man?" She tapped the image of Bradley Robinson. "Where did you get this?"

"Lesley gave it to me. Apparently, she's a tad better at researching than you. That," he said, tapping the photo, "is Bradley Robinson. Richard Robinson's younger brother."

"I do not understand."

"I'm not surprised. You never were the brightest bulb in the box."

Maria's eyes narrowed at him, but Steven didn't know whether she understood the metaphor he'd used. "I'll spell it out for you the same way Lesley spelled it out for me, okay? This man here." He tapped the photo again. "Richard Robinson? He is not your father. You see how this other man, Bradley Robinson, has his arm around your mother? That's your father."

"No." Maria shook her head. "Is not true."

"Yes, Maria, it is. Bradley Robinson knocked your mother up, and when he refused to do the right thing by her, Richard Robinson stepped in. Bradley Robinson didn't want you, but it doesn't matter because he died before you were born. His brother Richard saw to it that you and your mother were provided for, but Richard is not your father. He's your uncle. And as such, he doesn't owe you anything. So you can stop thinking you're going to get anything out of him, or Lesley, or anyone—"

"No!" Maria shrieked. She advanced on him around the counter. "You are lying."

She shoved at him, and it pissed Steven off. He set his drink down and shoved her back against the counter. "I am not lying," he told her through gritted teeth. "You've been lying to yourself. Nobody owes you anything, Maria. Richard allowed you to come here, to work in his house. He gave you a job and a chance, and you blew it—"

"No!" She shoved him again, harder, and Steven grunted when his lower back hit the counter behind him.

"Listen, you—"

She whirled away to the end of the counter, pulling a knife from the butcher block on the way. She turned and waved it at him, her face contorted in fury. "They owe me," she said in a guttural voice. "I am not some *puta* to be tossed aside."

Steven's own fury erupted. "Then stop acting like one, you little cunt."

She slashed out at him with the knife at the same moment he gave her another good shove, wanting nothing more than to get her away from him before one of them did something really stupid.

"Augh!" She'd managed to slice his forearm with the knife before she skidded backward in her ridiculous heels, losing her balance and crashing into the wrought-iron frame of the breakfast table, sending it into the wall, where the glass top cracked before it fell through the frame and shattered into a million pieces. The knife clattered across the floor.

Steven ran his arm under the faucet, keeping one eye on Maria in case she came after him again. She wasn't moving. He hoped she'd stunned herself good when she'd fallen. She didn't seem to be an immediate threat, so he dealt with his wound as best he could, wondering if he'd need stitches and, if so, how he'd explain such an injury.

He took a clean kitchen towel from a drawer and wrapped it tight around his arm, hoping it would be enough to stop the bleeding. Maybe he could get by with bandaging it himself later.

He looked once again across the room at the shattered table. Maria hadn't moved. While he stared, something dark and liquid began to seep across the tile. He watched in horrified, stunned surprise. Maria was bleeding.

Gingerly he stepped toward her, cradling his wounded arm next to him. He bent down, watching in sick fascination as a small pool of blood continued to spread out around her. Broken glass crunched under his shoes. He thought he felt her pulse flutter when he pressed his fingers against her throat, but then nothing.

Joy spurted through him before he could stop it. Maria Delgado was dead. She couldn't threaten him ever again.

Dread followed on joy's heels. Maria Delgado was dead. She was now a huge threat to him.

Chapter Twenty-Three

Steven's arm throbbed, making it hard to concentrate. He looked at the blood he knew would stain the grout in the breakfast nook tile. No matter what he did, what cleaning product he used, traces of Maria's blood would still exist. If a crime scene unit came in and spritzed luminol on it, even microscopic bits of blood might be detected. Then there was the glass. His DNA. Hell, his fingerprints on the body. Carefully he backed away.

He hadn't asked for much, had he? He'd wanted to be somebody, be a political player. Marriage to Lesley greased the wheels of that path. He'd been so close.

But Maria messed up his carefully planned strategy. Maria, with her innocent eyes and her subservient behavior. Her willingness to please him. He'd foolishly fallen into her trap. He hadn't seen the guile behind her eyes, hadn't suspected she'd set her sights high, just as he had when he'd married Lesley. He'd screwed her, but she'd screwed him even better. If not for her, he'd be a state senator by now with his eyes fixed on Capitol Hill.

Even though he was six years behind schedule now, he'd thought all of it was still possible. Certainly the state senate. He'd started from scratch, doing what he had to as an assistant in the state attorney's office, paying his dues, glad-handing the assholes who would someday support his run. Once again, Maria was about to ruin everything for him.

Even if he called 911 right now and explained the accident, the taint of a dead body—a young, attractive Latina whom he'd had connections with in the past—was not something he could overcome. He wasn't related to the Kennedys, nor was he part of the Robinson dynasty any longer. The political supporters who'd promised to back him would skitter away from him the way roaches ran from a light bulb. He might even lose his job.

They'd do an autopsy. They'd find his semen. He cursed himself for his lack of self-control. Hadn't he learned anything? With a shaky hand, he poured more Crown Royal over the ice melting in his glass.

He tried to think. Clearly. Quickly. At the moment it seemed he could do neither.

He'd already made the decision he wasn't going to call 911. Hadn't he? Yes. That meant he'd have to dispose of the body on his own. Somehow. Somewhere.

He'd have to clean up the mess. He'd have to point suspicion away from himself. As a prosecutor, he knew the best way to do that. Point it at someone else.

But who?

Steven thought of all the people he'd met in Willow Bay. He'd made a few enemies in his time. Rivals in his office certainly. Political opponents. Mostly, however, he'd done his best to survive by navigating the interconnecting spheres of his working and social life. He wasn't universally loved, of course, but he was usually able to keep his mouth shut and behave himself in and out of the office.

The last person who'd really gotten his goat was

that cop Lesley dragged to every formal affair this season. Niko Morales. Morales didn't seem to remember him, but Steven remembered Morales from the night about a year ago when the deputy pulled him over.

Spring break, and the beach bars in neighboring Fort Dunne were crawling with college kids getting drunk. Every year since his split with Lesley, Steven found easy pickings there. He'd single out a girl, separate her from the herd, and buy her a few drinks, and before long she'd agree to go home with him.

He'd been on his way to a cheap motel with a cute but pudgy blonde when he saw the swirling lights. Steven hadn't panicked. He wasn't drunk, although the girl was well past the legal limit. She found everything hilarious and hadn't stopped giggling since they left the bar.

He hadn't been speeding either, so why a deputy trailed behind him with his red and blues on, Steven couldn't imagine.

"Be quiet," he'd hissed at the girl, which only caused her to start giggling again.

He lowered his window as the deputy approached.

"Problem, deputy?" he'd asked.

"Can I see a driver's license and registration?" the deputy asked.

"Certainly." Steven extracted his wallet from his back pocket and reached into the center console for the registration. "What's the problem?"

"Hiya," the girl said, leaning across Steven's lap. "Wanna join the party?" She hiccuped before she started giggling again.

The deputy used a flashlight to check the

documents, taking his sweet time about it.

He flashed the light into the car at the girl. "She all right?" he asked.

"Fine," Steven snapped. "Too much to drink is all. I'm taking her home so she can sleep it off."

The deputy kept the flashlight on the girl until Steven said, "I'm a state's attorney, deputy. I suggest you tell me why you pulled me over before I consider filing harassment charges."

The deputy repositioned the beam so it was directly in Steven's face. Steven swatted it away. "Get that damn light out of my eyes."

The deputy complied. "That girl of legal age?" he asked in a calm tone.

"Of course she is," Steven spluttered.

"I'd like to see some ID."

"You're overstepping your boundaries."

"As a state's attorney, I'm sure you wouldn't want anything untoward to happen to a minor. Bad publicity and all that. Spring break's big money for the tourism industry, isn't it?"

Steven did his best to hide his irritation. His anticipation of an easy lay quickly turned sour. "You got ID?" he asked the girl.

Her head lolled back on the seat. "Sure do," she said in a sleepy, slurred voice. She tossed her wristlet at him.

Steven opened it and her ID was right there. He looked at it in the dim light. She was nineteen. He extracted the Indiana driver's license and handed it to the deputy. "Happy now?"

Deputy Morales checked the license with the flashlight. "Yes, sir. Thank you, sir. Reason I pulled you over is your driver's side taillight is out, and I wanted to let you know. I'm going to write you up a warning. You have ten days to get it fixed, or you'll be liable for the fine from the county."

"Fine." Steven seethed in silence while the deputy went back to his cruiser and wrote up the warning. Steven knew the deputy was also running his license and probably the girl's through the databases for any outstanding warrants or other red flags.

The girl snored softly in the seat next to him by the time Morales returned with the citation. He handed it, the IDs and the registration back to Steven. "Take care now. You have a good night."

Steven clamped down on the response he'd wanted to make. He stared at the signature on the citation. Niko Morales. It wasn't a name he'd planned to forget.

Perfect, he thought now. If only he could somehow frame Morales for Maria's murder. Murder? Where did that thought come from? Steven hadn't murdered her. True, he'd wanted to be rid of her, and now he was. But he hadn't murdered her. Her death was an accident.

But that didn't mean her death couldn't be made to look like murder. Blunt force trauma to the head. Her body dumped in a place that would throw suspicion onto someone besides Steven. Someone who looked like he was on the verge of getting everything he wanted, and therefore had a lot to lose.

Someone like Niko Morales.

That damned community center everyone was talking about the former gang member turned sheriff's deputy, had become the darling of the crème de la crème of the Willow Bay population. Not only that, he seemed to be Lesley's main squeeze.

The thought of Morales stepping into his former place in the Robinson family made Steven sick. Although he couldn't quite believe Lesley would actually marry someone so far below her social rank, she could be unpredictable. He'd never expected her to adopt his bastard child either, but that's exactly what she'd done.

Yes. Niko Morales would be the ideal candidate to frame for Maria's death. All Steven needed to do was figure out how to go about it. And soon.

Chapter Twenty-Four

Niko had to hand it to Kate Keller and Marsha Snyderman. They outdid themselves putting together the Salsa Bowl. Marsha's idea to use a local riding academy as a venue worked well. They'd rented a giant tent and a temporary floor beneath it. Round tables seating six were placed around the perimeter.

The academy building offered restrooms and a small kitchen. They'd put the bar along the walkway between the tent and the building so the ladies could avoid traipsing through the grass in their high heels.

Marsha and Kate thought of everything. They'd contacted dance academies as far away as Miami and Tampa, looking for instructors of both sexes, and hit the jackpot. There was no shortage of dancers willing to work the event for a nominal fee, mileage reimbursement, and the chance to promote their own classes.

A salsa band tuned up on the stage at one end of the tent. A hum of excitement buzzed in the air though it was still early. The caterers were setting up the buffet tables. Rather than a sit-down meal, the guests were invited to nosh on a variety of traditional Cuban, Caribbean, and Latin American foods.

There would be a silent auction for everything from dance lessons to a salsa cruise. Local restaurants, including Señor Tequilas, were on hand to supply at least one specialty to the buffet tables. Alicia made tubs of salsa for the event and donated cooking classes and gift certificates for meals at the restaurant.

Niko saw how this idea of his, which Kate and Marsha expanded on and ran with, became a community event. Some of the smaller specialty eating establishments were given an opportunity to showcase their cuisine and build their reputations and clientele.

"Everything looks amazing," Lesley said as she joined him near the entrance.

"Including you," he replied with a grin. Lesley wore a spaghetti-strap red dress that hugged her lithe frame and shone with spangles and beads. The long fringe covering the skirt swayed with her every move. Her hair was slicked back in a tight chignon adorned with a red hibiscus.

The compliment earned him a genuine smile of pleasure from Lesley. "Thank you. You look…wow!"

Niko chuckled. He'd chosen a long-sleeved black shirt and black slacks. It was simple and easy, and he knew he could carry it off better than a dance costume. Besides, the last thing he wanted to do was detract attention from any of his partners on the floor.

He and Lesley were manning the door as the official greeters, ticket takers, and hosts. Niko looked forward to seeing the couples he'd gotten to know over the course of the season, many of whom were now donors to the community center. This fun evening that he'd dreamed up was partly his way of paying back all the people who'd stepped forward to help him, who'd given him a chance. Even though they were also contributing even further to the cause tonight, he mainly hoped they relaxed and enjoyed themselves.

"It's all coming together, isn't it?" Lesley couldn't contain her excitement. She squeezed Niko's arm. "I can't believe you pulled this off in such a short period of time." She gazed at him in a more serious way. "I'm impressed."

"I had a lot of help," Niko reminded her. "I couldn't have done any of it without you or your friends."

"It might have taken you longer, but you'd have succeeded with or without me."

Niko didn't argue with her. Guests began to arrive, and it was time to play host.

****

Five hours later, the last of the guests left. The first Salsa Bowl had been, by all accounts, an overwhelming success. Niko fielded compliments all evening from the attendees. He'd given credit to everyone involved, because in his mind they did the lion's share of the work. He had simply been the instigator, and the community center the beneficiary. There were going to be a lot of sore feet in Willow Bay tomorrow, but this smaller, intimate affair gave everyone an opportunity to be involved in the various activities, lessons, and contests.

Niko and Lesley stayed for another hour, helping Kate and Marsha tie up loose ends, helping the caterers and restaurateurs load their vans and clean up. Lesley changed into a pair of low-heeled shoes. Her hair came loose from its chignon and tendrils curled appealingly around her temples and ears. The warmth of the late spring air combined with endless dancing took their toll. Even now he still felt a bit sweaty all over. Niko couldn't wait to get Lesley home, into the shower, and then into his bed.

Once he was on the road, behind the wheel of her Lexus, he took her hand and linked his fingers through hers. He brought the back of her hand to his lips for a kiss. "Thank you," he said, glancing over at her.

She rubbed her thumb along his, a smile on her face.

****

There was no question she would spend the night with him. She'd even packed a small overnight case.

"Let's take a shower," he suggested once they were inside.

"Perfect."

He turned the water on to let it warm up while they undressed in the bedroom. Lesley presented her back to him so he could unzip her dress. He marveled at their ease with each other as the dress slid off to pool at her feet. He kissed her shoulder, something he'd been wanting to do all night. With his arms wrapped around her from behind, he drew her up against his bare chest. He saw their reflections in the dresser mirror. The breath caught in his throat at her porcelain skin against his olive tones. Her blond hair and blue eyes contrasting with his almost black hair and equally dark eyes.

They were so different. Yet here they were together. For the moment anyway, he warned himself. Until Lesley got tired of the novelty of slinking around in secret and backed off. He didn't want to think about that. He nuzzled her neck, and she tilted her head back against his shoulder to give him easier access. He played his hands across her waist, sliding one down below the waistband of her lacy red panties and the other up to the matching strapless bra.

231

He teased her nipples through the material, feeling her sag against him. Her eyes were slits, but she watched their reflections too. He didn't know why it was such a turn-on, but he was hard and aching for release.

He maneuvered Lesley to the bathroom, where he dropped his slacks and adjusted the water temperature. She trailed a finger up between his buttocks while his back was to her. He turned around. "You'll pay for that."

"I hope so." Her eyes were dark, but she smiled. She unhooked her bra and let it drop. He grasped the waistband of her panties and yanked them off. She did the same with his boxers. "Oh, wow," she said when she saw his erection.

He helped her into the shower and got in right behind her, pressing himself up against her, feeling the sluice of the water run over her skin and onto his. There was no mirror in the shower, but the image of the two of them was still in his head.

He put his hands on her, one caressing her breasts and the other between her thighs, his fingers delving into the soft, wet heat of her. She was as turned on as he because she came quickly while his swollen cock still sought satisfaction.

She slid a hand back and grasped him before she turned. "How do we do this?"

He was lost in the feel of her hand on him and couldn't process the question.

"I know." She maneuvered around him so that he stood with his back under the spray. She bent forward and glanced over her shoulder. "Will this work?"

Niko's brain barely grasped what she offered, but

his body apparently knew what to do. He grasped her hips, spreading her for his entrance, and plunged inside. He couldn't suppress the groan of ecstasy that accompanied their joining from this angle. He found his rhythm, holding her in place, pounding against her, taking what she offered until he was spent.

His legs were jelly. His whole body felt like it might wash away along with the water swirling down the drain. His mind was mush. He brought Lesley up against him, holding on to her tightly, maybe even for support, while the water continued to pour over them.

Eventually, he shut the faucet off and grabbed a pair of towels, wrapping one around Lesley and the other around his waist. Together they stumbled to the bed and collapsed.

"That was…" Lesley murmured a minute later.

"Unbelievable," Niko finished for her. He lay on his back with his eyes closed and didn't think he had the energy to open them again.

But he smiled when he felt the press of her lips against his shoulder.

****

When Lesley woke, it was to Niko's touch. His hands and lips were everywhere at once, coaxing her body awake. She still felt ultrasensitive after their coupling in the shower. His teeth grazed her nipple, and she winced. Niko stilled. "What?"

"I'm just…I'm not…" She couldn't think how to explain.

He covered her body with his and played with a strand of her hair. "What?" he asked again, looking into her eyes.

Her body responded to his whether her mind

thought she was ready or not. "I feel very…" She looked away. Embarrassment got the better of her.

He brought her gaze back to his, turning her head with a finger against her chin. "Tell me," he whispered. His cock pressed against the dampness between her legs.

"It's stupid." She bit her lip. Since turning away hadn't worked, she looked down, allowing her eyelids to keep him from seeing into her too deeply.

"Lesley. Look at me."

She did. He was so close that even in the dim light she saw every detail of his face. His beard stubble, his beautifully shaped eyebrows, his sensuous lips. She traced a finger over his bottom lip without thinking.

"What is it?" he asked against her finger.

She gathered herself. "I feel a little…tender. Down there. From the shower."

He stared at her. "Did I hurt you? Tell me."

"No. I think it was…I don't know. It was different. You were very forceful." She smiled. "And very turned on."

"I'm always turned on around you." He wiggled against her to make his point. She sucked in a breath. He wouldn't have to do much more than he was doing to make her come. "I can wait."

"No!" She squeezed his shoulders. "Just be gentle. And go slow."

He smiled, his white teeth flashing in the gray shadows. "I can do that." He slid down, taking the sheet with him, and touched her very lightly with his tongue. Again and again. And again until she came in a soft ripple of sensation.

He entered her slowly, allowing her to adjust

around him. "Okay?"

"Perfect." She wished he would stay inside her and hold her tightly, just like this, for the rest of the night. She knew he couldn't. No man could. Well, maybe some could. What was it that Sting and his wife Trudy were famous for promoting? Tantric sex. Lesley made a mental note to investigate it.

"Want to be on top?" Niko asked.

"Maybe. But I'm not going to move if I am."

"Why not?" Niko rolled to his back, keeping her with him.

"Because this is just so lovely," she said sleepily. "Being this close to you. Having you inside me. Just...being."

****

Niko continued to stroke his hand up and down her back long after he knew she'd drifted into sleep. While he throbbed inside her, he thought about what she'd said. He'd have to wake her up, of course, and finish what he'd started. But for a minute or two longer, maybe he could give her what she wanted and just be.

Chapter Twenty-Five

Niko woke lying on his side in an empty bed, his arm stretched out across the rumpled sheets. Even though Lesley had stayed later than usual, that seed of disappointment lodged in his gut once again. They'd declared a silent truce after Niko's outburst on the beach, but he knew their relationship, such as it was, embarrassed her. She didn't want anyone to know she was sleeping with him, even if they suspected. Such a revelation would taint her carefully constructed public image.

He edged over to her side of the bed. He caught a whiff of her scent on the pillow, wished longingly that she were still there, even though it was midmorning and she was long gone.

What if she'd stayed, though? He'd make her coffee and toast. Bring it to her in bed. Wake her with kisses. They could make love in the light of day. Take another shower together. Go out to breakfast or something.

It didn't seem like asking a lot. Those were all simple things, weren't they? Maybe they were *too* simple. Lesley occupied a bigger world. She had an important place in it, running a Fortune 500 company, sitting on a board, arranging funding for needy causes.

What was he? A guy who came from nothing and who possessed very little even now. A small house, a used car, and a dream. He had a steady job and a desire to help others. That was about it. It wasn't much to offer someone like Lesley.

He rolled to his back and stared at the ceiling, which needed a fresh coat of paint. Ever since he'd met Lesley, it was like he'd stepped on a high-speed train without knowing where the tracks went. Sure, he'd been attracted to her from the moment they'd met, but she'd been so far out of his reach there'd been no point in even fantasizing about her. Not that it stopped him.

She'd turned the tables on him though, arranging it so they spent a lot of time together, and what was he supposed to do? Not be attracted to her? Not be interested in her? Not want to go to bed with her?

He'd done all that and more. He'd fallen for her. Then he'd done something stupid. He'd admitted it. She knew how he felt, and if he knew anything, he knew that was a cardinal rule a guy should never break.

He liked to think she shared these feelings, but there was a voice in his head warning him she might just be using him. Even if she did have feelings for him, she wasn't going to admit it to him or to anyone else. She'd never go public with their relationship. Inviting him to dinner at the manse had been the equivalent of throwing him a bone. She couldn't possibly believe they could have a future together. They were just too different. That their lives ever intersected at all was a minor miracle.

He saw it from her point of view. A public future together could negatively affect both of them. He'd be seen as a guy only after her money. She'd be seen as slumming, just like her ex-husband said at the Emerald Ball. She'd found someone to scratch her itch, that was all. Niko could imagine the ribbing he'd take if his relationship with Lesley became common knowledge and she eventually dumped him. Which she would.

He thought of the celebrities who'd had relationships similar to theirs. Powerful, wealthy women who "dated" unknown guys with questionable backgrounds and then unceremoniously dropped them. He did not want to be one of those guys.

Nope. What he should do was end this thing with Lesley, even if it would be like ripping his heart out. He'd probably never get over her. He'd heard people talk about the loves of their lives. Lesley was his. But there was no way this thing between them was going to last.

He'd hate like hell to lose the connection with Ricky as well. The kid needed a dad, or at the very least a male role model. Maybe Mitch could pick that up, although Niko was pretty sure he wasn't the only one who noticed Mitch was more interested in spending time with Mitzi than with Ricky.

Niko rubbed his hands over his face and got out of bed. At least the Salsa Bowl had been a smashing success. Kate would have the exact figures to him sometime this week, but she guessed they'd raised between ten and twenty thousand dollars.

Someone knocked on his front door as he finished washing up. He padded out to the front of the house in bare feet. Through the side glass he recognized a couple of the detectives from the sheriff's department. He opened the door.

Once they'd introduced themselves and gotten comfortable in his living room, the older one, Brandon Murray, began. "The body of a young woman was found in the field behind your community center."

Niko sat up, every sense on full alert.

"Formal identification is pending, but we believe it to be that of a young El Salvadoran named Maria Delgado."

They'd be watching him for any sign of recognition of the name, and Niko was pretty sure he hadn't been completely successful in hiding it. They'd caught him off guard, as they'd intended.

"When was she killed?" he asked, glancing from one to the other.

"We don't have an exact time of death," Murray said. "Right now the coroner believes she died sometime between one and three this morning. He should have a more exact time after the autopsy."

Niko breathed a shaky sigh of relief. He had an alibi for his time between one and three. Sort of. And a witness who knew exactly what he'd been doing during that two-hour window. Unfortunately, in order to clear him of all suspicion, she might have to sacrifice her reputation.

"Am I a suspect? Simply because she was found on the community center property?"

Murray and the other detective traded glances. "We believe death occurred elsewhere, and the body was dumped there. We would like to take a look around, with your permission, of course. To eliminate you from the suspect list. We'll also need to know where you were between one and three this morning."

"Do you have a search warrant?" Niko asked, knowing they didn't.

Again the trade of glances. "No," Murray said. "But we can obtain one if you'd prefer not to cooperate."

"Of course I'll cooperate," Niko informed them. "But I'd like to speak to an attorney before I do."

Chapter Twenty-Six

Lita tapped on Lesley's office door and stepped inside. She closed the door behind her.

"What is it?"

"Detectives from the sheriff's office. They're asking to see you."

"Detectives? What's it about?"

"They didn't say."

Lesley rose from her desk and followed Lita down the hall. "Detectives?" She crossed to where they waited in the foyer.

"Miss Robinson. I'm Detective Murray. This is Detective Peterson. We'd like to ask you a few questions, ma'am."

"In regard to?"

"Maria Delgado."

"I'll need more information than that if you want me to answer your questions."

A glance slid between the two detectives. Murray did all the talking. "Miss Delgado's body was discovered on the grounds of the Challenge Project's community center early this morning. We understand you're acquainted with the deceased?"

Body? Would the trip through Maria's haunted house of horrors never end? Lesley knew there could be land mines buried whichever way she stepped. Red flags popped up in her brain warning her to proceed with caution. With that in mind, she chose her words carefully. "She worked for my family several years ago."

"When's the last time you saw Miss Delgado?"

Lesley knew better than to answer questions like these without an attorney present. They might be only trying to reconstruct Maria's movements in the hours preceding her death, or they might be trying to find a suspect to charge with her murder.

"Detectives, I'll be happy to help with your investigation, but I'd like my attorney present during the interview. I'm sure you understand. Shall I have him contact you and set up a mutually convenient time?"

They weren't happy about it, but Murray handed over his card. "Please do. Thank you, Miss Robinson."

They left and Lesley's gaze collided with Lita's. "I have to make some calls."

The first one should be to Niko, to warn him. She hadn't asked when Maria's murder took place, but it was sometime last night. She'd spent the better part of it with Niko, which made him her alibi. And her his.

Lesley wouldn't have resorted to murder to get rid of Maria no matter how much she wanted the woman out of her life. Still, to rule Lesley out as a suspect, to rule Niko out as one if it came to that, the cops would require alibis from both of them.

Her stomach knotted while she waited for her attorney to pick up his phone. Her public relationship with Niko was well known. Her private relationship with him was still secret. She wanted to keep it that way. For now at any rate. When she was with him, she rarely thought beyond "now." She hadn't seriously thought about a future with him. She couldn't picture it happening, even though she could see herself with him forever. How would he fit into her life? Her lifestyle? How would she fit into his?

In her social circle, there was a word for what she'd been doing with Niko. She didn't care. He was a gentlemen. He was smart and sexy and driven. He'd overcome a lot in his life, and he'd developed character along with his natural charisma. So what if his annual salary was roughly what she spent replenishing her wardrobe each year?

I love him. Lesley could admit it to herself. But could she overlook everything she'd just mentally debated, the same things she'd been debating for months, and still be with Niko? For all time?

"Lesley? Sorry to keep you waiting."

"John. It's all right. I've got a problem. You remember Maria Delgado?"

"How could I forget?" John Cirillo had handled everything for her regarding Ricky six years ago. He'd kept it all quiet and confidential and smooth.

"She's been murdered. Detectives Murray and Peterson were just here from the sheriff's department. They want to interview me."

"She was killed here? In Willow Bay?"

"Yes. She's been here for several months, I believe."

"You've had contact with her?"

"Yes."

"All right. We need to talk first. Then we'll decide whether to set up an interview. What does your schedule look like for today?"

****

Lesley let herself into the suite of offices the Robinson Group maintained on Willow Bay's revitalized Fifth Avenue. On a quiet Sunday, the office was deserted, and so, for the most part, was the street outside. It seemed the best place to meet with Niko. She wouldn't risk a visit to his house or him coming to hers. Nor would she risk meeting him in a public place. Paranoia got the better of her since her visit from the detectives this morning. People were framed for murder all the time. Innocent citizens were sent to prison for years.

Her stomach twisted itself into a giant knot as she thought about everything her attorney told her when he'd called her back. A couple of neighborhood kids found Maria's body wrapped in a rug, surrounded by weeds, in the unpaved area beyond the community center's parking lot. The boys were taking a shortcut across the lot to the convenience store on the next street.

John set up a meeting in his office with the two detectives for tomorrow morning at ten o'clock. Lesley planned to meet with John at nine to discuss strategy.

The outer door opened, and Niko came toward her. Her heartbeat sped up the way it did whenever she was near him. She took in the expression on his face, serious but determined. Capable. Her stomach knotted further. There was a very good chance he was headed for a fall. Her addiction to him might ruin everything he'd been working for.

He stopped a foot from her and made no effort to come closer, either to greet her or embrace her. They studied each other before Lesley turned away, stepping back into the office and taking the chair behind the desk. Niko sauntered in after her, slumped into one of the chairs on the other side and trained his gaze on her face.

Having the desk between them bolstered Lesley's courage. She licked her dry lips. "We need to get our stories straight."

"There is no story. There's only the truth."

"I know. But the truth will ruin everything you've worked for. The truth will…"

"Ruin your reputation?"

"It will ruin *your* reputation," she snapped. "The slightest hint that I've shown some kind of favoritism toward the Challenge Project because of our personal relationship will not be good for either one of us."

"You're my alibi."

"And you're mine."

"Were you hoping I'd lie about us being together?"

Lesley hoped it wouldn't be necessary. Niko couldn't see what it would mean to both of them to have their private relationship made public. She saw by the look in his eyes that she'd taken too long to answer. "No."

"You don't sound too sure about that."

She'd seen Niko angry before. Seen his frustration. She saw those same emotions building inside him now. "I'd never ask you to lie. Especially not to save my reputation. I know you wouldn't do it to save your own."

"The truth sometimes has unpleasant consequences," he said. The anger and frustration she'd sensed before were gone. Thoughtfulness took their place. "But a lie… leads to secrets, which usually lead to something worse." He pinned her with his gaze.

Lesley didn't know if he was referring to his own past, to hers or to this very moment, but it seemed as though he'd just issued her a challenge. He was ready to face the consequences of going public with their relationship. Was she?

"I didn't kill Maria and neither did you. Maybe our best bet is to figure out who did. Who's got a grudge against both of us, and a big enough one against Maria that would make it worthwhile to see her dead?"

"She's only been in town for a few months. Who knows what she's been doing? But the only person I know she's had contact with and who might wish her harm is Steven."

"Exactly. Is he capable of it?"

"I hate to say this, but yes. Given the right set of circumstances, I think he could be."

"He's ambitious."

"Yes."

"Ruthless."

"Yes."

"Vindictive."

"We have no proof. We don't even know if Maria saw him that night or if he told her who her father was."

"If he did tell her, I bet he wasn't subtle about it. Maria was unpredictable. They might have argued. Maybe she came after him."

"Maybe," Lesley agreed. She knew firsthand how nasty and condescending Steven could be. How far he'd go to protect his own interests. It was all too easy to imagine the scenario Niko painted. "I agreed to be questioned with my attorney present. I suggest you do the same."

"I plan to."

"You have an attorney?"

"Yes."

Lesley couldn't hide her surprise. But Niko was a cop. Of course he'd know better than to do an interview without a lawyer present. "Good. I was going to make that nonnegotiable. I don't want you to lose everything you've been working for."

"I didn't do anything wrong," he reminded her as he came around the desk. "Except spend the night with you." He drew her up and looked into her eyes. "Remember that old song? 'If being with you is wrong, I don't want to be right.'?"

"I think it's 'if loving you is wrong, I don't want to be right.' "

"Yeah. That's it. Loving you. Come here."

Chapter Twenty-Seven

"Do you think he'll even let us in?" Niko asked as Lesley parked in a space near Steven's townhouse.

She peered up at his home. "I don't know. He might think it will look suspicious if he doesn't."

They made their way to Steven's door and rang the bell, listening to the chime echo inside. In less than a minute, Steven pulled open the door and stared at them.

"Lesley." He nodded at Niko. "What's up?"

"We'd like to speak with you for a few minutes," Lesley said.

"About what?"

"About Maria, Steven. Surely you've heard her body was found yesterday morning."

Steven folded his arms across his chest. "Yes, but I don't see what that has to do with me."

"Maybe nothing," Lesley said. "But both Niko and I have been questioned by detectives. We're under suspicion simply because we had contact with Maria. I would appreciate it if you'd give us a few minutes of your time and your expertise. That's all. We're a bit out of our element here."

Niko gave Lesley a lot of credit for playing to her ex-husband's ego. He practically preened at the suggestion that she was in need of his expertise.

Steven stepped back. "A few minutes is all I have." He directed them into the living room. Lesley perched on the edge of the sofa. Niko took one of the club chairs. Steven took the other.

"Now how is it you think I can help you?" he asked Lesley. He seemed perfectly willing to ignore Niko, which was fine with him.

"As I said, the detectives questioned us because we were in contact with Maria in the past few weeks. I'm assuming they plan to question everyone who did. Did you see her after we spoke the other day?"

"No."

"So you didn't give her the photo I gave you?"

"No."

"That means she didn't know Bradley was her father."

"Apparently not."

"It's funny. I thought she'd come to you again. Try to get you to help her."

"She didn't."

Niko knew Steven was lying. His answers were too clipped. Too professional. As a state's attorney, he'd surely cross-examined and coached hundreds of witnesses, done hundreds of interviews. He'd know to keep his responses short and sweet, direct and to the point. He had the distracted air of a man just hoping a problem would go away.

"You told me she kept coming around, asking for your help."

"Correct. Forgive me, but I don't see how questioning me about my interaction with Maria helps either of you."

"I'd hoped if she came to see you, maybe she let something slip, gave some clue about what she was going to do next or who she was going to see. Perhaps that would tell us how she died or who was responsible."

Niko admired Lesley's earnestness and concerned tone. Even though it was all an act. But it did the trick, Steven was practically jumping at shadows at this point. Niko cleared his throat, drawing Steven's attention away from Lesley. "Excuse me, man, but can I use your bathroom? Too much coffee this afternoon."

Steven gave Niko a look of irritation, but pointed. "Down the hall on the left."

"Steven," Lesley began as Niko made his way down the hall, "what do you think we should do? We didn't have anything to do with Maria's death, but—" Lesley's words died away as Niko closed the door to the half bath. He gave himself a minute before he flushed the toilet and opened the door, allowing the usual toilet noises to cover the sound of his footsteps heading for the kitchen. He glanced around at the open floor plan of the kitchen, breakfast nook and family room, then circled the kitchen island, looking for anything out of place.

The wrought-iron frame of the table in the breakfast nook was missing its glass. Four chairs were pulled up neatly around the empty frame. Niko's gaze dropped to the tile floor. It looked clean, except some of the grout showed an uneven, grayish stain. He glanced over his shoulder as he took the empty vial of luminol from his pocket and quickly pretended to spray it on the grout.

"What do you think you're doing?" Steven charged but stopped short when Niko straightened and held the bottle out toward him. "What the hell? I'm a state's attorney. You think I don't know my rights? Get out of my house, both of you."

"I've got a better idea," Niko said. "Why don't I call Detective Murray and invite him and his partner over? Tell them to bring CSU with them. What do you think will happen when they get a black light in here?"

Steven's gaze dropped to the tile. His face fell. His shoulders slumped. "They'd need a search warrant."

"They could probably get one easily enough, don't you think? If I mention the broken table, the stain in the grout, your connection to Maria?" He lowered his tone, the way he would to let a suspect know he had no way out. "They're doing an autopsy. You know the kind of tests they'll be running. How would you follow the trail of evidence?"

Lesley appeared behind Steven. Her gaze met Niko's. He nodded almost imperceptibly.

"Steven?" she queried in a hushed tone.

That seemed to be his undoing. He crumpled onto one of the bar stools, his face in his hands. "It was an accident," he moaned. "She cut me with a knife, and I shoved her away. Her head hit the table." He shook his head, still hiding his face in his hands. "I just wanted her to go away," he muttered. He sighed and lowered his hands. He stared out the window as if he was looking at something only he could see. "I just wanted her to go away."

Chapter Twenty-Eight

"We're ready for you, Ms. Robinson." Kelly Drummond, head of public relations for the Robinson Group, held open the door of the recording studio.

Lesley followed her into the booth. "Have a seat here," Kelly instructed. She patted the back of a burgundy leather desk chair. Lesley sat. She nodded at the cameraman, who was making adjustments to his equipment and the lighting.

Kelly stepped back behind the camera. "As soon as Charley's ready, we'll get started. We've fed your statement into the teleprompter, so just read it from there. I'll be keeping up with you. If you need to start over, just say so."

Lesley had been through this routine before. She'd done several podcasts for the Robinson Group website, usually around the time the annual earnings reports came out, or for some special media event or acquisition. As chairman of the board, she was the face of the company and its chief spokesperson. No one else could be given the responsibility of what she was about to do.

A few minutes later, Charley nodded to Kelly and Kelly said, "Ready?"

Lesley nodded. Charley counted down with his fingers, then pointed at her. She started reading.

"There has been a great deal of speculation

regarding my involvement in the death of Maria Delgado, a former employee of my family. Miss Delgado is suspected to be the victim of foul play, and her body was found on the grounds of the Challenge Project in Willow Bay, Florida.

"The Challenge Project is an organization dedicated to helping underprivileged youth in Willow Bay. It is a project I personally feel is worthwhile and that I personally support.

"I first learned of the project when Niko Morales, a deputy with the Waldon County Sheriff's Department, brought it to my attention. Mr. Morales wanted to present the project to the Robinson Family Foundation for funding.

"After a thorough investigation of Mr. Morales's background as well as the project's structure and viability, I recommended a presentation to the foundation's board. I was present at the presentation to the board. However, I abstained from voting for personal reasons. My vote was not necessary, in any event, as the other board members unanimously approved funding.

"Because I believed in the Challenge Project, I offered to introduce Mr. Morales to other individuals who might also be interested in funding the community center he had outlined as part of the project. Mr. Morales agreed to attend several social functions with me so that I could make these introductions. During the course of the time we spent together, Mr. Morales and I became friends, and later we became romantically involved.

"I did not want it to appear that the Challenge Project had been given preferential treatment over the many other funding requests being considered by the Robinson Family Foundation. Therefore, I suggested to Mr. Morales that we keep our involvement private. He agreed, as I am certain he was also under the impression that my reputation and by default that of the Robinson Group would suffer if we were to go public with our relationship. In short, I am certain Mr. Morales was concerned about the repercussions, both business and personal, were it to be known that the CEO of the Robinson Group was dating a local law enforcement officer.

"While I care deeply about the reputation of the Robinson Group, I refuse to allow my position with the company to dictate the choices I make in my personal life.

"I have decided to go public with our relationship for two reasons. First, Mr. Morales and I have both been questioned in regard to the death of Maria Delgado. I can say unequivocally that neither of us were involved and that the police are completely satisfied in this respect. But since the media will no doubt learn of our involvement during the upcoming trial of my former husband, keeping this relationship secret is no longer in the company's best interests.

"The second reason is because I love Mr. Morales, and I've been far too concerned about the reputation of the Robinson Group, as well as that of my family.

"And so I've come forward with a simple truth: Fear can keep us from living a complete life, just as surely as it can keep us from doing the right thing. This is my way of rejecting that fear. I hope if you ever find yourself with a similar dilemma, you will choose to do the same as I have."

"And out." Charley turned off the camera. The teleprompter stopped rolling.

"That was great," Kelly said, a slight tremor in her voice. She cleared her throat and came forward as Lesley stood. "We'll have this posted on the website shortly. We've set up the links for anyone who wants to view the Challenge Project's website or make a donation. I'll have my office field comments and questions or requests for interviews from the media."

"Thank you, Kelly. It's a relief to have this done."

"May I just say, Ms. Robinson, I admire you. A woman in your position, with your level of responsibility—it can't be easy."

"No, I don't suppose it is. But honestly I think I've made things harder on myself than they needed to be. Thank you again. We'll talk soon."

She strolled outside and was greeted by late spring sunshine. She breathed in the fresh air, looking forward to the summer and all it would bring. Humidity, thunderstorms, ninety-degree temperatures every day. She entertained herself with the thought of early morning runs on the beach with Niko. Rainy afternoons in bed with him.

As if she'd conjured him up just by thinking about him, she found him leaning against the hood of her car. She didn't even think about holding back her reaction. She smiled, letting her joy spill out.

"What are you doing here? How did you find me?"

He straightened as she came closer. "Your mother told me where you were."

She walked into his arms, and he kissed her. Oh, she could get used to this. Planned to get used to this. "I'm glad you're here."

"You are? Out here, where anybody and everybody can see us together?"

"Of course. I want them to."

"You do, huh? Not concerned what they'll think about a rich woman like you being with someone like me?"

"Not concerned at all. Because what they'll probably be thinking is how did that rich woman get so lucky?"

"I'm the lucky one," Niko said. He slid one hand into her carefully coiffed hair. With the other, he plucked the clip out of it and came in for another kiss. "So, so lucky," he whispered.

A word about the author...

Barista by day, romance novelist by night: When not writing fiction, Dr. Seuss-like poetry (for adults) or song lyrics, Barbara Meyers disguises herself behind a green apron and works part-time for a world-wide coffee company.

Her novels are a mix of comedy, suspense, and spice and often feature a displaced child.

Barbara is still married to her first husband and has two fantastic children. Originally from southwest Missouri, (she blames her roots in the Show Me state for her somewhat skeptical nature) she currently resides in Central Florida.

http://www.barbarameyers.com